Mistletoe Motel

A Sapphic Christmas Romance

Lise Gold

Copyright © 2024 by Lise Gold Books

All rights reserved.

No part of this book may be reproduced in any form or by any electronic or mechanical means, including information storage and retrieval systems, without written permission from the author, except for the use of brief quotations in a book review.

Edited by Debbie McGowan

Cover design by Lise Gold Books

Life is not about waiting for the storm to pass, but learning to dance in the rain.

— Vivian Greene

Chapter 1

Mack

The crackle of the airport's PA system cut through the low hum of conversation in Watertown Regional Airport's small terminal. Mack Harper looked up from her laptop, her fingers freezing mid-type.

"Attention passengers," a tinny voice announced, the speaker's forced cheerfulness barely masking their frustration. "Due to the winter storm, we regret to inform you that all flights scheduled for the next three hours have been cancelled. We apologize for any inconvenience. Please check with your airline's desk for rebooking options."

A collective groan rose from the scattered passengers. Mack slammed her laptop shut, shoving it into her messenger bag as she scrambled to her feet. She wasn't about to let a little snow keep her from making it to Minneapolis for Christmas. Her sister's baby was due any day now, and Mack had promised she'd be there.

She joined the quickly forming line at the airline desk, her hand instinctively moving to push back her teal-dyed hair. Tapping her foot impatiently, she glanced at her smartwatch and sighed. Yes, the storm was raging outside—in fact, she was lucky they were able to land here for her change over in the first place—but if she could just get on the next available flight, she might still make it home today.

Mack stepped up to the desk, flashing what she hoped was a winning smile at the tired-looking attendant. "Hi, any chance there's a seat left on the six-p.m. flight to Minneapolis?"

"You're in luck." The attendant tapped away at her keyboard. "We do have one seat remaining. Let me just—"

"Excuse me," a voice interrupted from behind Mack. "I couldn't help overhearing. Is there really only one seat left?"

Mack turned to see a young Asian American woman with a glossy black bob and dark eyes filled with worry.

"I'm sorry," the attendant said, "but yes, we only have one seat available in economy. And this passenger," she gestured to Mack, "is currently booking it."

"Please." The woman stepped closer to the desk, practically pushing Mack to the side. "I really need to get to Minneapolis. It's extremely important. Isn't there anything you can do?"

Mack felt a twinge of sympathy, but she squashed it down. "I'm sorry," she said, trying to keep her voice neutral, "but I also need to get to Minneapolis. It's important for me too."

"You don't understand. I have to be there for Christmas, and I'm a business-class passenger. I've paid more for my flight, so surely, that counts for something?"

Suppressing an urge to roll her eyes, Mack shook her head. "Everyone here needs to get home for Christmas, princess. Sorry. This seat is mine."

"Don't 'princess' me. How dare you! You don't know me." The woman's expression hardened. "Fine," she spat. "Enjoy your flight."

"I'm not sure what makes her think she's special," Mack mumbled to the attendant, who had watched the exchange with a weary expression.

"I heard that!" the woman yelled over her shoulder as she stormed off. "Karma's a bitch and you have it coming."

Mack sighed and ignored the comment. "I'll take the seat." Behind her, she heard sighs and curses from other passengers who would be stuck in Watertown. She'd be late for dinner with her family, but at least she would make it home.

As the attendant processed her booking, Mack glanced in the direction the woman had gone. She spotted her on the phone in a corner, waving her hands around, no doubt cursing her to whoever she was talking to.

"Here you go, Ms. Harper. Merry Christmas."

"Thank you. And Merry Christmas to you too." Mack shot the attendant a sympathetic smile as she gestured to the queue behind her. "I hope they don't give you too much of a hard time."

With her new boarding pass in hand, she searched for a place to wait for her flight, but with the airport at maximum capacity, all seats were taken and she had to settle for the floor. Leaving from Seattle this morning, it had been a long day already, but she figured she'd use her time wisely to tie up loose ends at work before Christmas.

As a software engineer for a promising tech startup, Mack had been working on an innovative AI-driven personal assistant app. The project was designed to anticipate users' needs based on their daily routines, calendar events, and even subtle changes in their tone of voice in order to assess their mental health. It was cutting-edge stuff, pushing the boundaries of natural language processing and machine learning.

The trip to Seattle had been to iron out some bugs in the speech recognition module. Mack had spent long days and even longer nights hunched over her laptop, tweaking algorithms and refining code. She'd made significant progress, but there were still a few persistent issues that needed addressing before the app could move to beta testing.

Half an hour crawled by, and then the PA system crackled to life once more.

"Attention passengers. We regret to inform you that due to worsening weather conditions, all remaining flights for today have been cancelled. The airport will be closing shortly. Our airline representatives will be available at the customer service desk to assist you with rebooking options and to provide information on discounted hotel rates for stranded passengers. We are working with local hotels to secure rooms, but please be aware that availability may be limited due to high demand. We apologize for the inconvenience and thank you for your understanding."

The announcement hit Mack like a punch to the gut. She sat there, stunned, as chaos erupted around her. Passengers rushed to the airline desks, voices rising in anger and desperation. But Mack knew it was pointless. Long queues were already forming, and by the time it was her turn, there wouldn't be any rooms left. She was stranded in Watertown, South Dakota, and she had to find a place to stay.

She pulled out her phone to call her sister, but the call wouldn't go through. "Great," she muttered, "cell towers must be down." The airport Wi-Fi was down too, and her hotel booking app didn't respond. While she kept trying to connect, Mack overheard fragments of conversations around her. Everyone was nervous about securing accommodations for the night. She heard mentions of the Watertown Inn, the Pine Lodge, something called the Mistletoe Motel, and several other motels outside town.

The reality of her situation crashed down on her. She needed to call her family, find a place to stay, figure out how to get to Minneapolis if the storm persisted tomorrow. Noting some people were already rushing outside toward the taxi stand, she decided she couldn't afford to waste any more time. Not in Watertown while hundreds of passengers were stranded.

The blast of icy wind nearly knocked Mack off her feet as she stepped outside. Snow whirled around her, reducing visibility to mere feet. The world beyond was a blank white canvas, the familiar shapes of cars and buildings obscured by the relentless snowfall. The biting cold stung her exposed skin, and she pulled her scarf up over her nose.

As she trudged toward the taxi stand, her boots crunched through several inches of fresh powder. The wind howled, drowning out the sounds of frustrated travelers behind her. Snowflakes clung to her eyelashes, and she blinked rapidly, squinting against the onslaught.

The yellow glow of taxi headlights pierced through the white curtain ahead, and she quickened her pace. The race for shelter was only beginning.

Chapter 2

Holly

Holly pushed open the door of the motel, a gust of icy wind following her inside. The warmth of the small lobby was a welcome relief, but the interior did little to lift her spirits. Her eyes were drawn to a tacky sign above the reception desk—*Mistletoe Motel* written in garish red and green letters.

"Welcome to the Mistletoe Motel," a cheery woman greeted her. "My name is Maude. How can I help you?" Maude lowered her reading glasses to the tip of her nose and peered over them. Her bleached perm sat atop her head like a tightly coiled cloud, each curl frozen in place, and she wore a sweater featuring a three-dimensional Christmas tree complete with actual tiny ornaments dangling from the knitted branches

"Hi, Maude." Holly suppressed a grin as she lowered her eyes to the nametag that said *Maude Mistletoe, General Manager*. "I need a room for the night." She brushed the snow from her coat. "Please tell me you have something available."

"That depends." Maude tapped at her computer. "We

only have Room Fifteen available, and that's because it's temporarily been taken out of our booking system. It needs repairs," she explained. "But considering the circumstances, we could rent it to you at a lower rate. At least you'll have a bed for the night."

"Great, thank you so much." Holly breathed a sigh of relief. After being turned away from two other hotels and an inn, she was starting to worry she'd end up having to beg strangers for shelter. "I'll take it," she said, reaching for her wallet.

As Maude processed her booking, Holly glanced around the reception area. "So, is it always the Mistletoe Motel?" she asked. "Or do you just change the name for Christmas?"

Maude chuckled. "Oh no, it's the official name. But the decorations don't go up until November. It adds to the festive cheer, don't you think?"

Festive cheer was certainly one way to describe it, Holly thought, taking in the overwhelming Christmas explosion around her. The lobby was a cacophony of clashing colors and mismatched decorations, as if Santa's workshop had vomited all over it.

The centerpiece was an enormous artificial Christmas tree that dominated half the space, its plastic branches sagging under the weight of countless ornaments. Tinsel in every shade imaginable was haphazardly draped over the tree, interspersed with blinking lights that seemed to be having seizures rather than twinkling merrily. At the top, a lopsided angel with a slightly sinister smile presided over the chaos.

The walls, barely visible beneath the decorations, were covered in faded wallpaper featuring a random pattern of pine trees. Strings of popcorn and cranberries zigzagged across the ceiling, intersecting with drooping paper chains and several pairs of stuffed elf legs sticking out as if they'd fallen through from the attic.

Every available surface was cluttered with an assortment of Christmas knickknacks. Snow globes of varying sizes crowded the reception desk, and a collection of nutcrackers stood guard along the windowsill.

The air was thick with the competing scents of cinnamon, pine, and what Holly suspected was a liberal application of Febreze to mask less festive odors. A small radio on the desk played "Jingle Bell Rock" at a volume just loud enough to be annoying.

The two plastic chairs in the waiting area hadn't escaped the holiday treatment either. They were draped with red and green covers, each adorned with a small wreath that had seen better days. Between them stood a tiny table offering a plate of cookies, disposable plastic cups, and a thermos.

Despite the overwhelming assault on her senses, Holly felt a twinge of amusement. There was something endearing about the sheer enthusiasm behind the decorations, even if the execution left much to be desired. It was clear that someone—probably Maude—had poured their heart into creating this winter wonderland, however misguided the result might be.

The door behind her swung open, letting in another blast of cold air, and Holly turned to see a familiar face—the woman from the airport, the one who got the last seat on the flight to Minneapolis. Her beanie and teal hair sticking out from underneath it were dusted with snow, her cheeks flushed from the cold.

Their eyes met, and Holly felt a mixture of emotions—frustration at her situation, a twinge of guilt for how she had acted at the airport, and, she had to admit, a bit of smug satisfaction. Karma, indeed.

She turned back to Maude, taking her key card. "Sorry," she said to the newcomer, unable to keep a small smile from her face. "Last room."

The woman looked like she was about to burst into tears. "Are you sure?" she asked Maude. "Is there anywhere else I can try? All flights have been cancelled. The airport's closing."

Maude shook her head. "I doubt it. By now, the hotels in town are booked solid with stranded travelers."

"What about a rental car?" she asked, desperation creeping into her voice. "I could try driving to the next town."

"Car rental's closed by now," Maude said. "And even if it weren't, driving in this weather would be madness, but don't worry. There is another option," she offered. "The church is providing shelter. You'd have to sleep on the floor, but at least you'd be safe and warm. They'll have coffee and cake too. They're always prepared to welcome stranded travelers during storms."

Mack nodded slowly, seeming to accept her fate. She turned to leave, and Holly was struck by how defeated she looked. A wave of conflicting emotions washed over her. Part of her wanted to relish in this karmic twist, a petty revenge for the woman's earlier behavior at the airport. But as she watched Mack's shoulders slump, guilt began to gnaw at her. Holly thought about her own relief just moments ago when Maude offered her the last room. She imagined spending the night on a cold church floor, surrounded by strangers, while outside a blizzard raged. It wasn't right. Yes, the woman had been rude earlier, but did she really deserve this? Besides, she'd been rude herself, and fair was fair. She'd been behind her in the queue, and it wasn't just Holly who needed to get home for Christmas.

Holly's mind raced, weighing her desire for a peaceful night alone against her conscience. She thought about her parents—devout Christians who had taught her to always help those in need. What would they think if they knew she had left someone out in the cold?

With a mix of reluctance and resolve, Holly made her decision, and before she could change her mind, she called out to her. "Wait..."

The woman turned back, surprise on her face.

"Does the room have one or two beds?" Holly asked Maude.

"There's one bed." Maude smiled. "But it's king-size. Are you willing to share?"

Holly took a deep breath, hardly believing what she was about to say. "Sure. It's only one night." She met the woman's eyes and shrugged. "If you want."

The woman's eyes widened and she stared at Holly for a beat, as if gauging if this was some cruel joke.

"I mean it," Holly assured her, then pointed to the window. A taxi was pulling up and people were rushing out. "Make up your mind before I offer it to someone else."

"No, I'd love to," the woman said quickly. "Thank you, that's so kind of you. I'd be very grateful. I just...you know, after what happened at the airport, I didn't think you'd..." She bit her lip and winced. "Anyway, we can talk about that later. I'm Mack."

"Hi, Mack. I'm Holly." She wasn't looking forward to sharing a bed with her, but it wasn't like it could get any worse, and part of her wanted to show Mack that she wasn't a *princess*.

Maude let out a shriek of joy and clapped her hands

together. "Now that's the Christmas spirit!" She prepared another key card and handed it to Mack. "We don't serve food, I'm afraid, but there's a convenience store nearby, and I'll ask housekeeping to bring some extra coffee, tea, and instant cocoa to your room. She's on her break now, but she'll be back shortly."

"Thank you, Maude. You've been amazing." Holly hesitated as she swung her weekend bag over her shoulder. "Just out of curiosity...what's wrong with the room? Is the toilet in working order?"

"Yes, the toilet and electrics should be fine," Maude said. "Just some damages to the interior, but nothing that will keep you from a good night's sleep." She leaned in, lowering her voice. "And don't you worry about a thing, girls. Either my husband or I will be at the front desk all through the night. If you need anything at all, just come on down and we'll take care of you."

Chapter 3

Mack

Mack followed Holly through the snow-covered parking lot, her boots leaving deep imprints in the fresh powder. The storm was intensifying, and she could barely make out Holly's figure a few steps ahead, leading the way to their shared room.

As they reached the door marked "15," Mack noticed the peeling paint and the slightly crooked number.

Holly fumbled with the key card before finally managing to unlock the door, and they stumbled inside, grateful for the shelter from the storm.

Mack's relief was short-lived, however, as she took in the state of the room. The first thing that caught her eye was the writing above the bed. Someone had scrawled DON'T FALL ASLEEP in large, foreboding letters directly onto the faded floral wallpaper.

"Okay..." she mumbled. "That's seriously disturbing."

"Totally," Holly agreed. "I guess now we know why this room was out of the booking system."

There was a suspicious-looking hole in the wall that had been poorly patched. The curtains hung crookedly, one partially detached from its rod. The next thing Mack noticed was the size of the bed, or rather the lack of size.

"Um, Holly?" she said, frowning. "That definitely doesn't look like a king-size bed."

The bed in question was barely larger than a standard double, its sagging mattress and threadbare comforter a far cry from what Maude had promised. "Are you sure about this? I can sleep on the floor if you'd prefer. I don't want to make you uncomfortable."

Holly blew out her cheeks and shook her head. "It's no problem. It's just for one night. Besides, I'd feel terrible making you sleep on this floor. You might end up with a skin disease." She gestured to the stained carpet. "It's gross. I'll make sure to keep my shoes on while I'm walking around."

Mack grinned. "Thanks. I promise I don't snore...at least, I don't think I do." The bedside lamp flickered ominously when she turned it on, casting eerie shadows across the walls. The bathroom door didn't quite close all the way, leaving a gap that promised little privacy.

As Mack hung up her coat, she noticed another small hole in the wall next to the door, and peering closer, she realized she could see into the next room. Two people, both naked, were sleeping on the bed, face down. There was a half-empty vodka bottle on the nightstand and their clothes were strewn over the floor. "I think we have a peephole situation here."

Holly came over to investigate and grimaced. "Looks like they had a fun time." Without hesitation, she removed the chewing gum from her mouth and deftly pressed it into the peephole, effectively sealing it. "There. Lucky for you, I'm a problem solver. What bothers me most, though, is that writing on the wall. It's giving me serial killer vibes."

"I'm not too worried." Mack suspected whoever wrote it had been high as a kite. "The town feels safe. It's not like we're in a motel along a deserted highway, but..." She smiled as an idea formed in her head. "I suppose they'll redecorate the wall anyway, so if it makes you feel better..." She rummaged through her backpack and pulled out a thick, black marker. With a few strategic additions, she transformed the ominous message into DON'T FALL ASLEEP WITHOUT FLOSSING. "Better? Lucky for you, I'm a problem solver too."

Holly burst out laughing. "That's brilliant. And somehow even more disturbing. I feel like my dentist is haunting me now."

"At least you won't forget to floss," Mack quipped, laughing along. The howling wind outside reminded them of the storm, and she moved to the window, pushing aside the crooked curtain to peer out. The parking lot was now completely blanketed in white, the snow showing no signs of letting up. "I was hoping for a white Christmas, but this was not what I had in mind."

"Looks like we're really stuck here," Holly murmured. "What a bizarre situation."

Mack nodded. "Let's hope the airport reopens tomorrow, and if it doesn't, I'll just rent a car."

"Was Minneapolis your final destination?" Holly asked.

"Yeah. I live there. You?"

"Same. It's crazy to think that we're only a four-hour drive away and there's no way we can get there tonight." Holly looked deflated as she said it, but Mack didn't pry. She didn't know Holly and suspected she might not want to share her personal story as well as a small bed.

As silence fell between them, Mack became more aware of the room's odor. The stench of stale cigarette smoke mingled with the sour smell of spilled alcohol that had seeped deep into the carpet fibers over time.

"God, it reeks in here," she muttered. "Mind if I open the window for a few seconds? Just to air it. I suspect that hasn't happened for a while."

Holly nodded, wrinkling her nose. "Please do. It's pretty bad."

Mack wrestled with the old frame, and it finally gave way with a loud crack, but her triumph was short-lived. A gust of icy wind burst into the room, sending the curtains flying and nearly ripping the already precarious curtain rod from the wall. Snow swirled in, immediately dampening the carpet near the window.

"Shit!" she yelled, changing her mind and struggling to close the window against the force of the storm. Holly rushed to help, and together they managed to slam it shut.

"Okay, bad idea." Mack panted, looking sheepishly at Holly, who was dusted with snow. "I guess we'll have to cope with eau de cigarette and booze. Maybe it'll grow on us?"

Holly laughed, brushing snow from her hair. "Yeah, nothing says 'Christmas' quite like the aroma of a frat party aftermath. But hey, at least now we know the window actually opens. That's got to count for something in this place."

Mack was relieved that Holly took the situation in stride. "Silver linings, right? I should probably head out to the convenience store to get us some supplies before it closes. I'll add Febreze to the list. What can I get you?"

"Are you sure? I can come with you, it's—"

"No," Mack interrupted her. "It's terrible out there. There's no need for both of us to walk through the storm." Checking her phone, she noted the signal was still weak.

"And I should probably call my family from the landline at reception to let them know I'm stranded."

"Yeah, I'll do the same," Holly agreed. She pulled a few bills out of her pocket and handed them to Mack. "I'll scan the room for other peepholes while you're away, so if you could get me more chewing gum, that would be great. I'm almost out."

Mack chuckled. "Of course. What else? Do you drink? Want to share a bottle of wine? Any allergies?"

"Yes to the wine. I really need a drink after today," Holly said. "I prefer red, but I like a dry white too. And I don't have allergies, so take your pick for the food, as long as you bring me some salted pretzels."

"No problem. Pretzels and red wine coming up." Mack put on her coat, her scarf, and her beanie. "Thanks again for sharing the room. I know I wasn't exactly nice to you at the airport. I'm not normally rude."

"Forget it. I was worse." Holly walked over to Mack and readjusted her scarf, pulling it all the way up to her chin. "Stay warm, and if you can't see where you're going, just come back. We can always raid the vending machine for candy."

The scarf thing was curiously intimate for a stranger, and Mack inched back a little, creating more space between them.

"And I promise you, I'm not a princess," Holly added, meeting her eyes.

Mack stared at her for a beat. Holly certainly looked like a princess with her shiny, dark hair and flawless skin. She was one of those women who were incredibly beautiful without trying, or perhaps not even knowing it. "I didn't mean that," she said, then shook her head and chuckled.

"Okay, maybe I meant it in the heat of the moment, but now..."

"Now that you've got a bed, I'm not so bad, huh?" Holly arched a brow and shot her a playful smile.

"No, you're not." Mack studied Holly more closely and felt a flicker of curiosity about her new roommate. She caught herself staring and quickly looked away, suddenly aware of how fragile their situation was. It wasn't the time to be admiring her temporary roommate's good looks; the last thing she wanted was to make Holly uncomfortable.

"I should get going," she said, zipping up her coat. "I won't be long."

Chapter 4

Holly

Holly had just finished lighting candles when Mack walked in with a smug smile, her arms laden with bags.

"Honey, I'm home," she called, her voice tinged with humor.

Holly laughed. "Welcome back. The Wi-Fi is still down, but I found a blurry TV channel that plays Christmas music. It drowns out the noise of the storm and the neighbors, who just woke up. They're currently having a row over who drank more of the vodka and should therefore go out in the storm to buy more."

"Why am I not surprised?" Mack set the bags down on the small table by the window and began unpacking their makeshift dinner. "Did you do that for me?" She gestured toward the candles Holly had placed around the room.

Holly rolled her eyes, the corners of her mouth tugging up into a smile. "Sorry to disappoint you, but no. I went to call my family and asked Maude for candles. That flickering bedside lamp was driving me crazy, and the overhead light is bright enough to perform surgery under, so I figured we needed something more subtle."

"Good call. I'm not a fan of bright lights either." As Mack continued to unpack, Holly watched with growing amusement. Out came crackers and cheese, a pot of raspberry preserve, two wilted ready-made salads, two slices of old pizza, salted pretzels, a candy bar, two bottles of red wine, water, napkins, paper cups, air freshener, and two wooden forks.

"Quite the feast you've assembled there," she remarked, eyeing the spread.

"Only the finest dining for the princess who gave me a bed for the night. Oh, and I got us this too." Mack pulled out a deck of cards. "In case you're up for some entertainment that doesn't involve staring at that 'don't fall asleep' message all night."

"That's really sweet of you. I do enjoy a game of gin rummy."

"Excellent. So do I." Mack smirked. "And I promise I'll stop calling you princess now. Unless you want me to?"

Holly felt a sudden warmth creep up her neck at Mack's playful comment. Was she flirting with her? She took a moment to really look at her, taking in her teal-dyed hair, her infectious smile, the humorous sparkle in her blue eyes, and the confident set of her shoulders. Mack was attractive and Holly suspected she was gay; her radar was rarely off.

It had been a while since she'd allowed herself to flirt with anyone, but then again, this whole situation was far from normal, and a little harmless flirtation might not be such a bad thing. After all, they were stuck here together, and it could be a fun way to pass the time and take her mind off the fact that she couldn't get home.

"Well," she finally said, "I suppose I could get used to being called princess. As long as you don't expect me to wear a tiara to bed."

Mack's eyebrows shot up, a grin spreading across her face. "No tiara required. Though I bet you'd look good in one."

"Careful now," Holly teased as she pulled back one of the seats at the table, "or I might start to think you have ulterior motives." The chair wobbled as she sat down and she almost fell off, eliciting another burst of laughter from both women.

"Oh yes, because nothing says romance like a dingy motel room with questionable wall art and a peephole to the next room." Mack folded one of the paper shopping bags and wedged it under Holly's chair leg to stabilize it. "I'm so sorry I'm not living up to your romantic expectations, princess."

Holly felt a flutter in her stomach at her new nickname and focused on opening the wine. "Well, you did bring me wine and pretzels. That's a good start." She poured them both a cup and opened the bag of pretzels.

"Don't forget about the wilted salad and the pizza that's been sitting under a heated lamp for most of the day." Mack sat opposite her, topped one of the salads with a slice, and scooted it across the table.

Holly picked up her slice and attempted to take a bite. The crust was so hard she winced as she took a bite, then struggled to chew it.

Mack, watching Holly's struggle, picked up her own slice and tapped it against the table. The sound it made was more akin to a rock than food. "We're going to need a Christmas miracle to eat this," she said humorously. "But thankfully, I brought two bottles of wine, so we can use that to wash it down."

They both laughed, clinking their paper cups together in a mock toast to their culinary misfortune.

"So, Mack, what were your plans for tonight before you ended up here?" Holly asked. "Did you manage to get in touch with your family?"

Mack nodded, taking a sip of her wine. "Yeah. My sister was pretty disappointed, but she understands. It's not like I can control the weather."

"You were visiting your sister?"

"She's due to give birth tomorrow, on Christmas Eve," Mack explained. "That's why it was so important for me to get home."

Holly winced. "Fuck. I'm so sorry."

Mack nodded, taking another sip of wine. "Yeah, it's... it's not ideal. This is her first child, you know? I promised I'd be there for her."

"You could still make it. The weather might clear tomorrow and—"

"But it's not going to clear, though, is it?" Mack interrupted. "Maude told me the weather forecast is getting worse by the minute."

"Hmm..." Holly sat back and sighed. "Yeah, she told me the same."

"What about you?" Mack asked. "You seemed pretty desperate to get on that flight. Family waiting?"

Holly hesitated, swirling the wine around in her glass. She wasn't sure how much she wanted to share, but something about Mack made it easier to open up. "Yeah, family," she finally said. "My parents. We've had some...issues lately. This Christmas was supposed to be about reconciliation."

She took a deep breath. "I came out to them in January. It didn't go well."

Understanding dawned on Mack's face. "Oh... That must have been really hard."

Holly shrugged, trying to appear nonchalant despite the ache in her chest. "We're getting there. They're trying, and Mom has asked me to spend Christmas with them, which makes me think they're willing to talk about it and maybe even accept it now."

"That's really positive," Mack said. "Do you have siblings?"

"No, it's just me and my parents." Holly sighed. "The thing with being an only child is, the expectations are enormous. In my case, their expectations were for me to get married to a man, buy a home, have babies, and meet them at church every Sunday. It's unlikely any of that will happen, so needless to say, they need some time to get used to the idea. I don't understand why they were so surprised in the first place. I've never shown any interest in men, and they even caught me kissing my best friend when I was twelve."

Mack chuckled. "Ah...the best friend. Haven't we all been there? My parents were very accepting when I came out to them, though. I was lucky that way."

Holly felt a blush creep up her cheeks when their eyes met. "You too, huh?"

"Yeah. I'm gay too. But don't worry. I'll stick to my side of the bed," Mack joked.

"So will I," Holly quipped with a wink. "So do you have a girlfriend? Wife?"

"No, I'm single." Mack ran a hand through her hair, leaving it tousled. "You?"

"I'm single too. I was seeing someone, but she left me right before I came out to my parents. She didn't want to date someone who was in the closet. She'd been through that before with her ex and didn't like that we always had to spend the holidays apart." Holly shook her head. "I was so hurt, but it also gave me the courage to come out to my parents. I knew I had to if I wanted to win her back."

"But that didn't work out?" Mack asked.

"No. A month later, I called her to tell her the news, but by then, she was already seeing someone else. Considering how fast she moved on, it clearly wasn't meant to be."

"So you've been struggling with your breakup and your parents," Mack said.

"Yes. I'm over my ex, but I want my family back. I need them in my life."

Mack reached across the table to squeeze her hand. The gesture was simple, but it conveyed a depth of understanding that Holly hadn't expected from someone she'd only met hours ago.

A gust of wind rattled the window, drawing her attention to their reflection in the glass. The sight made her chuckle softly.

"What's so funny?" Mack asked, tilting her head.

Holly gestured toward the window. "I was just thinking about how we must look to anyone passing by. Two women sharing a candlelit dinner of convenience store delicacies in a worn-down motel room. It's like the setup for a bizarre indie film."

Mack grinned as she turned to look at their reflection. "Oh yeah, I can see it now. *Stranded at the Mistletoe: A Christmas Tale of Dental Hygiene and Unexpected Friendship.*"

"Starring two lesbians who started out as enemies and ended up sharing a bed," Holly added, laughing.

As their laughter subsided, Holly realized she wasn't all that miserable. Yes, she was stuck in a questionable motel room with a stranger. But somehow, it didn't feel as dire as it should.

Chapter 5

Mack

Mack leaned back against the headboard, wine glass in hand, trying not to stare too obviously at Holly. They had finished their makeshift dinner and decided to get more comfortable, settling onto the bed with the remaining wine. Holly wore an oversize T-shirt that rode up slightly, revealing a tantalizing glimpse of her thigh. Mack found her eyes drawn to it repeatedly, each time forcing herself to look away.

"So," Holly began, swirling the wine in her glass, "have you always lived in Minneapolis?"

"Pretty much, other than college. How about you?"

"Same, though I was born in South Korea. I was adopted as a baby by my parents here in the States. They're Minnesotans through and through."

"Oh? You're adopted?" Mack wasn't sure why that surprised her. Maybe because she'd never met anyone who was adopted. "How was that, growing up?"

Holly tilted her head from side to side, her expression turning thoughtful. "It was tough at times. I always felt different, you know? I stood out, and kids can be cruel. There were times I wished I looked more like my parents or the other kids at school." She paused, reaching for a pretzel.

Mack watched as Holly dunked the pretzel in her wine before eating it.

"And then realizing I was gay on top of that," Holly continued, "it was a lot to process. I didn't want to be different in yet another way."

Mack felt a pang of empathy. "That must have been really hard. How did you finally come to terms with it?"

Holly shrugged. "Time, I guess. And meeting other queer people who helped me see that being different wasn't a bad thing. It's still a journey, but I'm getting there."

"And your parents? You mentioned they're quite religious?"

"Yeah. They're kind, loving people, but their faith is a big part of their lives. It's been difficult for them to reconcile their beliefs with who I am. I'm not religious anymore. I decided a long time ago it wasn't for me, but I still go to church with them sometimes, just to keep them happy. Well, I used to before we fell out, anyway. We've spoken on the phone, but I haven't seen them in almost a year, even though they only live a half-hour drive away from me."

"Are you nervous?"

"Very," Holly admitted. "But they've taken a step in my direction, so I have to meet them in the middle. It's up to me now, I guess." She turned to Mack. "Anyway, enough about me. Tell me more about your family. Your sister who's about to give birth—do you know if it's going to be a boy or a girl?"

"No, they've decided to keep it a surprise. My sister says there are so few true surprises left in life, she wants to experience this one fully."

"That's sweet." Holly reached for another pretzel, and again, Mack watched as she dunked it in the wine. "Okay, I have to say something." She pointed to the bag of pretzels. "That's just weird, what you're doing."

"What?"

"Soaking the pretzel in the wine. Who does that?"

"Oh." Holly laughed. "I'm a dunker. I dunk everything. You should see me with cookies and hot cocoa."

"Yeah, but that makes sense. Dunking in wine, however..."

"Why?" Holly stared at Mack as if *she* were the odd one out. "They're both going to end up in my mouth eventually. I might as well combine them before they enter. You should try it. It's good."

"Before they enter," Mack repeated with an amused smile. "I will have you know I chose that wine carefully. It's a nice bottle and you're polluting it with your pretzel crumbs."

Holly rolled her eyes and held out the bag. "What? You're a wine snob?"

"Would you be surprised that a woman with brightly colored hair likes good wines?"

Holly took a moment to consider that. "Yes," she finally said. "I would have never taken you for a wine connoisseur, and I know," she continued, holding up a hand, "I shouldn't judge a book by its cover. Not that I think you look..." She winced and let out a nervous chuckle. "I mean, I think you look great. More than great, just not like the type to...never mind. I'm digging a hole for myself here, so I'll shut up."

"Well, I am very much a wine connoisseur." Mack felt amused as she watched Holly blush. It was cute. Just as cute as the pretzel-dunking, but she was not going to give Holly the satisfaction of telling her that. "This particular bottle," she said, lifting it, "is a 2018 Château Bellevue Bordeaux. It's a blend of Merlot and Cabernet Sauvignon, with notes of black cherry and a hint of oak. Not exactly what you'd expect from a convenience store, right?"

"Uhm...I don't know." Holly was clearly clueless.

"Just take my word for it," Mack said. "It was hidden behind a bunch of cheaper bottles on the top shelf and covered in dust. They must have had it for years."

"Was it expensive?" Holly asked.

"Not really. Forty dollars for a bottle like this is a bargain, although it hurts me to drink it from a paper cup."

"Forty dollars seems a lot for a bottle of wine from a convenience store," Holly said, glancing down into her pretzel-clouded drink. "Paper cups and pretzels. Did I make the hairs on your back rise? I guess I owe you some more money too..."

Mack laughed. "No, this one's on me and the dunking... It's cute," she said before she could stop herself. "I mean, I..." She swallowed hard, cursing herself. Now she was the one stammering.

"You think I'm cute?" Holly joked teasingly, batting her eyelashes.

Mack felt her face grow hot as she fumbled for words. "I mean, not cute like... I didn't mean... It's just the pretzel thing is...endearing?" She winced, realizing she was only making it worse.

A smirk played at the corners of Holly's mouth. "Endearing?"

"No, I mean yes, but..." Mack took a deep breath, deciding to just bite the bullet. "Look, you're attractive, okay? Like, really attractive. Pretty. Beautiful, even. I'm not blind." The words tumbled out in a rush, and Mack wanted to hide under the bed.

Holly's eyes widened slightly, her smirk transforming into a genuine smile. "Oh," she said softly. "Thank you."

Mack plowed on, unable to stop her undoubtedly destructive verbal diarrhea. "And it's not just your looks. You're smart and funny, and the way you eat pretzels is weirdly captivating, and I know we just met, and this is probably incredibly inappropriate given our situation, but... yeah. You're cute. In an objective, stating-the-facts kind of way."

There was a moment of silence as Holly absorbed this clumsy confession, and Mack held her breath, mentally kicking herself for potentially ruining the easy camaraderie they'd developed.

Finally, Holly spoke. "Well, for what it's worth, I think you're pretty cute too. In an objective, stating-the-facts kind of way, of course."

Mack let out the breath she'd been holding. "Oh. Good. I mean, not good, but...you know what I mean."

Holly laughed, the sound breaking the tension. "We're quite the pair, aren't we? Stranded in a motel, sharing a bed, and now awkwardly complimenting each other."

Mack couldn't help but join in the laughter. "Yeah, this is definitely not how I expected today to go."

"Me either," Holly agreed, reaching for another pretzel. She held it up, a mischievous glint in her eye. "So, wine snob, want to try my 'endearing' pretzel-dunking technique?"

Mack pretended to consider it seriously. "Well, I suppose in the spirit of new experiences..." She took the pretzel from Holly, their fingers brushing lightly in the exchange. Mack tried to ignore the little jolt that ran through her at the contact. She dipped the pretzel into her wine, eyeing it dubiously before popping it into her mouth. Chewing thoughtfully for a moment, she finally nodded. "Okay, I hate to admit it, but that's not half bad."

"See? I told you." Holly smirked mischievously. "Sometimes the best combinations are the unexpected."

Chapter 6

Holly

Holly glanced at the clock and was surprised to see how late it had gotten. They'd talked about their lives and their jobs. Mack had enthusiastically described her work as a software engineer, explaining her current project developing an AI-driven personal assistant app. In turn, Holly shared about her career as a corporate lawyer, specializing in mergers and acquisitions. She told Mack about her recent trip to Seattle, where she'd been negotiating a complex deal between a local start-up and a major tech company. They'd both been surprised to discover the overlap in their professional worlds, with Holly often working with tech companies and Mack's company potentially being the kind that Holly might represent in the future. The conversation had flowed easily, and they'd lost track of time as they shared stories of challenging projects and workplace anecdotes.

"We should probably try to get some sleep," she suggested reluctantly. "I want to get up early to check on available flights or rental cars, even though there's only a slim chance we'll get lucky." She was enjoying herself and didn't really want the night to end, but at the same time, she felt the weight of the day catching up with her.

Mack stifled a yawn. "You're right. I'm tired too. We could always rent a car together? It's quite a distance. It would help to share the driving."

"Yeah, I'm up for that." Holly liked Mack's sleepwear—a pair of soft-looking sweatpants and a form-fitting tank top, and she found it hard to keep her eyes off her toned arms, the muscles shifting subtly as she got out of bed and headed for the bathroom.

Holly hesitated for a moment before following Mack into the bathroom. The small space felt even more cramped with both of them in it, and she was acutely aware of their proximity. She reached for her toothbrush, her hand brushing against Mack's arm in the process. Focusing on the task at hand, she tried to ignore the way her heart raced every time Mack's elbow bumped against hers. She was usually so composed, so in control of her emotions, but something about Mack threw her off balance in a way that was both terrifying and exhilarating.

How had this woman, who she'd been ready to throttle at the airport, become someone she wanted to be close to? Holly shook her head, trying to clear it. It was unlikely they'd ever see each other again after they returned home, so it wasn't worth breaking her head over.

"Don't forget to floss," Mack mumbled through a mouthful of toothpaste. She winked, meeting Holly's eyes in the mirror, and it brought a flutter to Holly's core. There had been a shift in the atmosphere. Their earlier confessions of finding each other "objectively" attractive hung in the air between them, creating a new tension, and she felt self-conscious, hyperaware of every movement she made.

She studied Mack's face, noticing details she hadn't

before. The way Mack's blue eyes crinkled at the corners when she smiled, the small scar just above her left eyebrow, the splash of freckles across her nose that were barely visible unless you were looking closely. Mack's teal hair was messy now, giving her an endearing, tousled look.

Just hours ago, she'd been yelling at Mack, and now she found herself desperately wanting Mack to like her. It was a strange sensation, this sudden desire for approval.

After they finished up in the bathroom, Mack paused at the foot of the bed. "Are you absolutely sure you don't want me to sleep on the floor? I really don't mind," she offered again.

"I wouldn't dream of it. We'll manage just fine in the bed."

"All right, if you're sure. Just promise to tell me if I start snoring or hogging the blankets." They moved around the room, extinguishing the candles one by one. As the last flame flickered out, darkness enveloped them, broken only by the faint glow of the lights outside, filtering through the thin curtains.

When they settled into bed, Holly was acutely aware of Mack's presence beside her. The bed, which had seemed small earlier, now felt impossibly tiny. She could feel the heat radiating from Mack's body, hear the soft sound of her breathing. Holly lay still, trying to regulate her own breaths, feeling as though every small movement was magnified in the darkness.

The mattress, worn from years of use, dipped noticeably in the middle, creating a subtle slope that threatened to draw them toward the center. She'd noticed it sitting up before, but now it was so much harder to stay on her own side. She tensed her muscles, trying to maintain her position on the edge of the bed, fighting against the pull of gravity.

After a few minutes of silent struggle, Mack's voice broke through the darkness, tinged with amusement. "I'm starting to think this bed is conspiring against us," she said dryly. "It's like trying to stay on a hill without rolling down."

Holly chuckled, relieved that she wasn't the only one struggling. "I was just thinking the same thing. This bed is basically a relationship accelerator."

"Well..." Mack's voice was softer now. "I suppose there are worse things than ending up in the middle. At least we won't fall off the edges."

Holly's heart rate picked up at the implication. She took a deep breath, deciding to let go of her resistance. "You're right. It's probably easier to just go with it."

Slowly, they both allowed themselves to slide toward the center of the bed. Their backs met in the middle. Holly's skin tingled everywhere where they touched—the press of Mack's shoulder blades against hers, the slight contact of their hips, the way their legs just barely brushed against each other.

"Are you comfortable?" Mack whispered.

"Yeah." Holly's mind began to wander, unbidden fantasies creeping into her thoughts. She imagined Mack turning around, facing her, and in her mind, she could almost feel Mack's lips on hers, soft and insistent. The imaginary kiss deepened, and Holly felt a rush of heat course through her body.

She squeezed her eyes shut, trying to banish the thoughts but failed. The attraction she felt was undeniable, and if she were ever going to have a one-night stand, this would be the perfect opportunity. They were already in bed together, unlikely to ever see each other again after tomorrow. The attraction was mutual; Mack had admitted as much earlier.

But what if Mack for whatever reason rejected her advances? The thought of facing her tomorrow after an awkward encounter was enough to keep her paralyzed with indecision, as she lay there, hyperaware of Mack's every movement.

All Holly had worried about lately was her parents, waiting for her in Minneapolis. The reconciliation she hoped for, the conversations that needed to be had. There was none of that going through her head anymore and instead she was entertaining thoughts that would surely shock her conservative family.

The irony wasn't lost on her. Had the universe thrown this curveball her way? Part of her wondered if this was some sort of test of her resolve, or maybe just her self-control.

Mack's breathing deepened into the steady rhythm of sleep, but Holly was unable to drift off. Despite the wine and the long, exhausting day, her mind refused to settle. Every small sound seemed amplified—the creak of the bed, the rustle of the covers, the distant howl of the wind outside.

Mack shifted and turned around in her sleep, and Holly felt the warmth of her body as she moved closer. Without warning, her arm slid around Holly's waist, and she snuggled up against her back.

At first, Holly stiffened, her mind racing with thoughts. Did Mack mean to do that? Was she just pretending to be asleep? Should she move away? But as Mack's warmth seeped through the thin fabric of her shirt, Holly finally relaxed into the embrace. It was so long since she had been held like this, so long since she'd felt this kind of closeness. She allowed herself to sink into the moment, savoring the feel of Mack's arm around her, the steady rise and fall of her chest, the soft brush of Mack's breath against her neck.

Tomorrow would bring new challenges—the struggle to get home, the uncertainty of what this meant. But for now, in this unlikely sanctuary they'd found in a shabby motel room, Holly finally allowed herself to simply be. She drifted into dreams filled with teal hair, soft touches, and the lingering warmth of a kiss she had yet to experience.

Chapter 7

Mack

The hot water pounded against Mack's skin as she stood under the shower, trying to scrub away the mix of embarrassment and arousal that clung to her. She couldn't shake the memory of waking up half on top of Holly, her arm draped over her waist. The realization had jolted her awake, and she had scrambled out of bed, praying Holly hadn't noticed. Now, under the steady stream of water, she tried to clear her mind.

After a few more minutes, she sighed and turned off the shower. With her skin flushed from the heat, she quickly dressed, then took a deep breath, steeling herself before stepping out of the bathroom.

Holly was up now, standing by the window with the curtains open, sipping a coffee. The morning light filtered through the thick snowfall, casting a soft glow around her. She turned to Mack, her eyes fluttering over her.

"Come and have a look," she said. "I've never seen so much snow."

Mack crossed the room and joined her by the window. The world outside was pristine white, the cars buried under a thick blanket of white. The snowfall was still heavy, but it had transformed the landscape into something out of a winter fairy tale.

"It's beautiful," she admitted, her eyes tracing the delicate patterns of frost on the windowpane. But as much as she appreciated the picturesque scene, she sincerely wished the snow would stop. Every flake that fell felt like another obstacle keeping her away from her family and the birth of her niece or nephew.

Holly nodded. "I made you a coffee." She pointed to a paper cup on the table.

"Thank you." Mack stirred some sugar through it. The cheap instant coffee was bitter, but she still savored her first caffeine hit.

"Did you sleep well?" Holly asked, a hint of mischief in her smile.

Mack felt herself blush, unsure how to answer. "Uh, yeah. Did you?"

"Like a log." Holly's smile widened. "You know," she continued, her tone teasing, "you were getting really cozy with me."

"Uh..." Mack stammered, desperately searching for a way to change the subject. "I, um, didn't mean to—"

"Don't worry, it was nice," Holly interrupted her with a chuckle. "Just, next time, maybe buy me dinner first?"

Mack's blush deepened, and she was about to make a fumbling apology when a knock on the door saved her. She nearly leapt at the distraction, grateful for the interruption. She opened the door to find a cleaner standing there, her arms full of sachets of instant hot cocoa and coffee, and a large storage box.

"Good morning," she greeted them. "Maude asked me to bring these. She also wanted me to decorate your room since it's the only one that hasn't been done, in case you're staying another night."

"Oh..." Mack shook her head. "That's very sweet, but we're leaving today. Decorating isn't necessary."

The cleaner looked doubtful. "With the airport closed until tomorrow and the roads in this condition, I think you might be stuck for a bit longer. But by all means, you should try. Maude will have a list of local rental companies."

Mack's heart sank at the thought of being stuck longer. "All right," she said, turning to Holly. "Why don't you take your time in the shower? I'll get dressed and call the car rentals at reception. If I manage to get one, we can share."

"Thanks. I won't be long." Holly turned to the cleaner. "By the way, can you tell us about the peephole situation?"

"Yeah, sorry about that." The cleaner chuckled. "Room Fifteen is for watching, and Room Fourteen is for people who like to be watched. Watertown Motel is kind of famous for it; all. All the locals know about it. We don't give out these rooms unless people specifically ask for them, but with the weather situation, Maude had to make use of the space she had, and I guess she forgot to mention it. I see you've already taken care of it, though," she added, noticing the chewing gum in the hole.

"Okay...so it's a thing," Holly said with a frown.

"Oh, you'd be surprised." The cleaner looked amused. "We had two couples who booked both rooms for a whole week. They switched places every night." She glanced up at the wall. "I like what you've done with the wall art. I've seen some interesting things here, but that's a first. Creativity is definitely appreciated. Makes it way less creepy somehow."

"We improvised. I hope Maude doesn't mind."

"Of course not." The cleaner put down the box. "Are

you sure you don't want me to decorate while you're out? I assume you'll go for breakfast?" She held up a hand when Mack was about to protest. "I know, I know. You're hoping to get out of here, but my shift finishes at ten and I'd hate for you to miss out on Christmas decorations in case you don't manage to get a car."

Mack hesitated for a beat, then gave in. "Sure. Thank you. Just give us some time to get ready and the room is all yours." She didn't care for Christmas decorations, and she had no intention of staying if she could help it, but the cleaner was clearly passionate about it, like everyone else in this establishment, it seemed.

"Great." The cleaner beamed and saluted her on her way out. "I think you'll be pleased to see how even the dreariest of rooms can be transformed."

Mack put on her coat and shoes, and glanced at Holly, who gave her an encouraging smile. "Good luck with the car rentals," she said.

"Thanks." She braced herself and opened the door to a gust of icy wind. The snow was deep, and each step was an effort, but she made her way to the reception.

Inside, Maude greeted her with a cheery smile and an interesting Christmas sweater with a frontal view of a reindeer, its eyes made of big, golden baubles. "Morning, dear! How did you sleep?"

Mack forced a smile. "Good morning, Maude. I slept well, thank you. The cleaner told me the airport will remain closed today, but we really need to get to Minneapolis. She said you have a list of local car rentals? I can't get a decent enough signal on my phone to look them up."

"I certainly do." Maude handed her a short, handwritten list. "But I have to warn you, many of the cars were rented out yesterday afternoon after the first flights were canceled." She pushed the phone in Mack's direction. "Here, use this one."

Mack's heart sank a little, but she thanked Maude and started making calls. There were five car rentals in and around Watertown, and each conversation was the same: no cars available, everything rented out, and the roads were too dangerous to drive on anyway, so what was she even thinking?

Holly joined her just as she hung up from the last call. "Any luck?" she asked, though her hopeful expression faltered when she saw Mack's face.

"None at all," Mack said, her voice heavy with disappointment. "I don't know what else to try."

Holly sighed. "Well, all we can do is make the best of it, I suppose." She turned to Maude. "Is the room free for another night?"

"Already done," Maude said with a wink. "I've been through enough blizzards to predict the aftermath, so I took the liberty of reserving it for you."

"Thank you." Holly gave her a half-hearted smile. "I'll call my parents. Let them know I'm stuck here for Christmas Eve."

"I'll do the same. And then we should probably get some decent food," Mack said. "Anywhere we can get breakfast around here, Maude?"

"Oh, yes! My brother's diner does the best pancakes. And it will be open tonight too. He's serving traditional Christmas food. You'll also have better luck with the Wi-Fi there. It's usually pretty stable."

"Thanks. What's your brother's diner called?"

"It's the Mistletoe Diner," Maude said. "We're an entrepreneurial family, us Mistletoes."

Mack stared at Maude as she processed the information. It sounded like a joke, but she suspected it wasn't. "Wait... Is Mistletoe your real surname?"

Maude chuckled, her eyes twinkling with amusement. "It sure is. I'm Maude Mistletoe, the eldest sister. My brother, Marty, runs the Mistletoe Diner, and our younger sister, Millie, runs the gas station. It's only a five-minute walk from here. She sells great gifts."

Holly exchanged an incredulous glance with Mack. "Well, that's certainly memorable. We'd better check it out. Oh, and thank you for the room decorations. That's very kind."

"You're welcome, girls. No one escapes Christmas in Watertown, stranded or not."

Chapter 8

Holly

The plate clinked in front of Holly, and she looked down to see a stack of blueberry pancakes arranged to resemble Santa's face. His beard was made of whipped cream, his eyes were blueberries, and his hat was made of pre-molded red Jell-O. "Thank you. This looks..."

"Weird?" the waitress finished her sentence, then lowered her voice as she glanced over her shoulder. "I know. My boss insists we do this every year. It's a pain in the ass. Santa's eyes keep rolling off and the cream melts all over the plate."

Mack, seated across from Holly, couldn't stop laughing. "Looks like Santa's been having some skin issues," she joked, pointing to the blue-tinged pancakes.

Holly laughed along and noted Mack's breakfast was no less elaborate. Her omelet was shaped like a Christmas tree, complete with green spinach leaves for the tree and tiny red and yellow pepper pieces as ornaments. "I have a feeling this town takes Christmas very seriously," she said, shaking her head in amusement. "Or maybe it's just the Mistletoes."

"Oh, you've met them? Are you staying at the motel?" the waitress asked.

"Yeah, we've met Maude," Holly said. "She's lovely. An interesting character."

"They all are." The waitress sighed. "There's no escaping the Mistletoes during the festive season. You can't swing a candy cane without hitting one of them. It's like they hibernate all year and come December, they multiply and take over the town." She brushed her hands on her apron and straightened herself. "Well, enjoy your breakfast, and brace yourselves for Marty."

As they dug into their breakfasts, Marty, the overly enthusiastic owner of the Mistletoe Diner, bustled around, greeting every customer with a hearty "Merry Christmas!" He approached their table, scratching his grey beard with a huge smile on his face. "Morning, ladies! You must be Holly and Mack. Maude told me you'd be coming. How are you enjoying Watertown's hospitality?"

Holly smiled as she looked up at him. Clearly, the love for Christmas sweaters ran in the family. Marty's was riddled with sewn-in twinkling lights. "Everyone's been really sweet," she said. "And your decorations are really something."

The diner was a riot of Christmas kitsch. Tinsel and fairy lights were draped across every available surface, and Christmas music played loudly over the speakers. A large tree stood in the corner, adorned with mismatched ornaments and a slightly crooked star. The booths were decorated with festive seat covers, and each table had a small poinsettia centerpiece.

Marty beamed with pride. "Glad you like it! Here, have some hot cocoa." He placed two steaming mugs in front of them, each topped with a generous swirl of whipped cream and a candy cane.

"Thanks, Marty," Mack said, lifting her mug in a toast. "This looks delicious."

"Hot cocoa on the house for everyone today," he said, then nodded toward the window. "Hey, what do you think about all the snow? Isn't it amazing?"

Holly didn't have the heart to disagree with him, so she painted on a smile. "It sure is. I've never seen so much snow before."

"You have to check out the Watertown snowman competition later today," Marty continued. "We have some real talented people in the community and anyone can join." He clapped his hands together as two new patrons entered the diner. "Oh! Duty calls. Enjoy your stay, ladies!"

Holly tried to keep a straight face as she met Mack's eyes. "All drama aside," she said, "I have a feeling this will be a Christmas to remember."

"It already is." Mack shot her a goofy grin as she dug into her breakfast. "What did your parents say when you told them you weren't coming?"

"They were disappointed." Holly speared her fork through one of Santa's eyes and dipped it in the whipped cream. "Especially Mom. She said they could try to pick me up, but I told them not to. I don't want them to drive in this weather."

"No, best not," Mack said.

"Anyway," Holly continued, "there will be many more Christmases, but there won't be another chance to witness the birth of your niece or nephew. It's much worse for you. If there was any way of getting home and only one person could go, I'd want it to be you."

"Thank you. That's very sweet." Mack smiled sadly.

"Maude was right. The signal's fine here. I just got a message from my sister and she's not showing any signs of labor yet. No contractions, water still intact." She chuckled softly. "Maybe the little one's holding out for Aunt Mack to arrive before making their grand entrance."

"Well, babies are notorious for ignoring due dates," Holly said. "There's still a chance you might make it in time. How's your sister holding up?"

"She's doing okay," Mack replied, taking a sip of her cocoa. "Just really over being pregnant at this point. She says she can't wait to finally meet the baby and stop feeling like a walking incubator. At least they live close to the hospital. Apparently, it's snowing pretty hard in Minneapolis too, so that's one less thing to worry about." She shrugged. "So, let's just try to make the best of it. I might pick up my laptop and try to get some work done."

"Work?" Holly's eyes widened. "You can't work, it's Christmas Eve!"

"Hey!" Mack chuckled as she held up a hand. "Don't go all Mistletoe on me. I was only going to check my emails."

"No one is working today." Holly jutted out her bottom lip. "Besides, what am I going to do all by myself if you're buried in work?"

"Okay, okay. So what do you want to do, princess?"

Holly laughed and slapped her playfully on the arm. She secretly liked her new nickname, but Mack didn't need to know that. Mack arched a brow and Holly was pretty sure there was something suggestive in her gaze.

"Well, how about this? We could walk through town and check out the sites and the snowman competition first. If you're worried about your signal, we'll ask businesses if we can use their landline and you can call home every hour to check."

"We could do that..."

"Great!" Holly clapped her hands together. "Have you ever built a snowman before?"

"It's been a while, but I'm in. It sounds fun." Mack glanced at her over the rim of her cup as she sipped her cocoa. "And then what?"

Holly narrowed her eyes and paused while she continued to work out an itinerary. "Then, we head over to the gas station," she said. "It makes sense, right? We can't miss out on the third Mistletoe enterprise. It's a must."

"Totally." Mack grinned. "So we'll hang out at the gas station for a while? This sounds like the Christmas of my dreams already. Please continue."

Holly laughed at her dry sense of humor. "Hang on. I hadn't finished." She tore off a piece of pancake and dunked it in her hot cocoa. "Maude said her sister sells gifts, so we'll pick out a small gift for each other that we can exchange over dinner tonight. And while we're here having a Christmas meal, we can videocall our families."

"Okay." Mack stared at her with an amused twinkle in her eyes. "I love your plan. A snowman competition, a gas station visit, a romantic Christmas dinner at the Mistletoe Diner and virtually meeting the parents. This relationship is certainly speeding up considering we started out on the wrong foot."

"I don't know about romantic," Holly said, glancing around. "It's more like a Hallmark movie on a budget."

"Hmm... Yeah, you're right." Mack inched forward. "Think about it. Two strangers, stranded in a quirky town, forced to share a room, frolicking in the snow, and sharing a cozy meal." She stole a piece of Holly's pancake, dunked it in her cocoa and continued to stare at her. "And then what happens?" She chewed slowly, licking her lips.

"Then..." Holly swallowed hard. The way Mack's eyes darkened made her heart race. The playful banter between them was turning more intimate with each passing second and she didn't know what to do with herself. "Have I turned you into a dunker?" she asked, pointing at Mack's cocoa in an attempt to distract herself from that sexy stare.

"Maybe." Mack tilted her head and arched a brow. "But you're changing the subject."

Holly sat back, creating some space between them. "You're pretty direct, aren't you?"

"I can be. I'm sorry. Is it too much?"

"No," Holly admitted after a moment's hesitation. "I guess we'll just have to see where the night takes us."

Chapter 9

Mack

Despite the heavy snow fall, the town square was bustling with people. The main road had been cleared, but the storm still made it challenging to walk. Mack pulled her scarf tighter around her neck, her breath visible in the frigid air. The town seemed undeterred by the weather, its spirit lively and cheerful.

In the center of the square was a Christmas market, featuring little German-style chalets with vendors that sold food, drinks, and various holiday trinkets. Children ran around, their laughter mingling with the jarring festive music playing in the chalets. The aroma of mulled wine, freshly baked cakes, and roasted chestnuts wafted through the air, tempting passers-by to stop and indulge.

Mack and Holly wandered through the market, taking in the sights. The chalets were decorated with twinkling lights and garlands, each one more charming than the last. She watched as a vendor poured hot cocoa into a mug, the steam rising and dissipating into the frosty air. There was an ice-skating rink, currently closed as it wasn't safe to skate in the weather, but it looked charming, nevertheless, with its rustic wooden fence adorned with twinkling fairy lights. Red and green garlands intertwined with the lights, and a large Christmas tree stood in the center of the rink, its branches heavy with snow.

"Over there!" Holly's voice called out, snapping Mack out of her reverie. She gestured to a chalet that said *Snowman Competition. Sign up here!* "Are you ready to build the winning snowman?"

"You bet!" Mack's competitive spirit was already kicking in as she eyed up their competition. Both kids and adults had gathered in groups with bags full of props and accessories.

"We should have come prepared," Holly whispered as they signed up. "They clearly take it very seriously."

"That's okay. We can improvise. I—"

"All right everyone!" a woman interrupted them. "Gather 'round so we can go over the rules. I'm Barbara, your competition leader."

The group shuffled closer, and Mack could feel the buzz of anticipation.

"The rules are simple," Barbara said, the jingle bells around her neck tinkling with every movement. "You have forty minutes to build your snowman. You can use up to five props—no more. Props include anything you add to your snowman that isn't snow. That means buttons, hats, scarves, accessories, and so on. You'll be judged on creativity, craftsmanship, and overall holiday spirit," she continued. "Because the spirit of Christmas is just as important as the snowman itself. So put your hearts into it!"

Holly grinned, her eyes meeting Mack's. "We really have landed in a Hallmark movie."

"And one last rule," Barbara added, raising her hand for emphasis. "The cheesiest rule of all. Have fun!"

Mack and Holly headed to their designated area, marked by a sign with their number. The ground was packed with fresh snow, perfect for molding. Mack crouched down and began scooping snow together for the base, and beside her, Holly started with a small snowball, rolling it across the snowy ground to gradually increase its size.

"I'll shape the legs, if you do the body and the head base," Mack said, patting down the pile of snow in front of her.

"Got it," Holly replied, working methodically. "It seems like everyone has a plan, but what are we even making? Santa?"

"Yeah, why not? Let's keep it simple." Mack glanced around, her eyes scanning the ground for anything they could use as props. A few feet away, she spotted a broken candy cane half-buried in the snow. She picked it up, dusting off the snow. "We could use this as a pipe. What do you think?"

"Perfect! Holly chuckled, her eyes lighting up with excitement. "The beard will be easy to mold, and I'll try to find something that could work as a hat."

They continued building, their hands moving swiftly as they shaped the snowman. Holly formed the midsection and the head, smoothing out the surface while Mack sculpted the legs, making sure they were sturdy enough to keep the body in place.

Mack couldn't remember the last time she'd had so much fun. The simple act of building a snowman—something she hadn't done since she was a child—filled her with a kind of innocent glee she had long forgotten. She glanced at Holly, who was grinning from ear to ear as she packed out the snowman's body. Her enthusiasm was infectious, and she looked adorable with her cheeks pink from the cold.

Holly disappeared for a moment and came back with two twigs.

"I found a pair of arms!" she called out, holding them up in triumph.

"Great. They're beautiful claws," Mack joked, sticking the left one in while Holly attached Santa's right. Holly adjusted them so they were symmetrical before they molded Santa's beard and stuck the pipe into his mouth.

Mack stepped back and admired their work with a smug smile. "Not bad, huh? We just need a hat."

"I'll be right back," Holly said, running off again. She returned with a red tinsel garland and a Santa hat. "I bought this at one of the stalls," she said, holding up the hat. "And the wind blew the garland into my face like it was meant to be."

Mack wrapped the tinsel scarf around the snowman's neck while Holly placed the hat on its head.

"Santa's got a great butt," Holly noted as she walked around their snowman. "Very perky. Let's hope they take that into consideration with the scoring."

"Oh, are you a butt person?" Mack asked teasingly.

"I do appreciate a nice butt. Yours is great, by the way," Holly shot back at her.

"So is yours." Mack playfully slapped Holly's behind, making her jump and laugh. "I was admiring it when you were looking out the window this morning."

"Oh yeah? Were you checking me out?"

"Guilty." Mack shivered at the surge or arousal that coursed through her. This was getting interesting "I wouldn't mind seeing a little more of it," she said, hoping she wasn't taking it too far. "It really is quite something. You know, in an objective, stating-the-facts kind of way."

Holly rolled her eyes and laughed. "Oh, that again?" She bit her lip as she looked Mack over. "Well, keep up the charm and you might get lucky."

Mack's jaw dropped as she stared at her. "You're going to drive me crazy, you know that?"

"Good," Holly replied, batting her eyelashes. "I've been told I have that effect on people." For a moment, they simply stood there, facing each other, and Mack's pulse quickened as fantasies coursed through her mind.

Just then, a countdown began from the crowd. "Ten! Nine! Eight!"

Holly's eyes widened in a panic. "We forgot the eyes and the nose! How could we forget those?"

Mack snapped out of her reverie and started digging in the snow until she found two rocks. "These will have to do," she said, bursting into stitches of laughter as she pressed them into Santa's sockets.

In a wild frenzy, Holly ran around, looking for a nose.

"Five! Four! Three!"

"I can't! This is too stressful." Failing to find anything suitable, Holly turned to the contents of her purse and pulled out a bright-red lipstick. She rolled it all the way out and jammed it into the middle of their snowman's face, just in time.

"Two! One! Time's up!" Barbara screamed.

Mack and Holly stepped back, both crossing their arms over their chests as they surveyed their creation in mock seriousness. The snowman stood at a precarious tilt, its body formed of unevenly packed snowballs that gave it a distinctly lumpy appearance. The rocks they'd used for eyes were hilariously mismatched—one oversized and the other barely more than a pebble—giving it a comically bewildered expression. Holly's bright-red lipstick, repurposed as a nose, jutted out like a clown's honker.

"Well, there he is," Mack said, stifling a laugh.

"Yeah..." Holly shook her head, giggling. "I think we nailed it. He's got personality, that's for sure."

Chapter 10

Holly

"I can't believe we came last," Holly said, shaking her head in disbelief as she and Mack trudged through the snow toward the Watertown gas station. "Our Santa was clearly the most anatomically correct snowman in the competition."

Mack snorted, her breath visible in the cold air. "Yeah, I'm sure that's exactly what the judges were looking for. 'Most accurate snowman gluteus maximus.' It was—" She paused, squinting through the heavy snowfall. "Wait. Is that...is that the gas station?"

Holly followed Mack's gaze and felt her jaw drop. Even from a distance, the gas station stood out like a beacon in the storm. It was as if Christmas had exploded all over the building, leaving no surface undecorated. Strings of multi-colored lights outlined every edge and window, blinking in dizzying patterns. A massive Santa waved cheerfully from the roof, flanked by a team of lit-up reindeer. The gas pumps hadn't escaped the festive treatment either; each one was wrapped in tinsel garlands and topped with a small Christmas tree.

"I guess we know where Maude and Marty get their decorations from," Holly said, pushing open the door and setting off a cacophony of jingle bells.

The interior was even more overwhelming than the exterior. Every inch of space was crammed with merchandise, creating narrow aisles that wound through the store like a maze.

"Welcome to Millie's!" a cheerful voice called out. A woman who could only be Millie Mistletoe emerged from behind a tower of Christmas sweaters, each more garish than the last. She bore a striking resemblance to Maude, but where Maude's enthusiasm was tempered with a touch of world-weariness, Millie seemed to operate on another frequency entirely.

"What can I help you ladies with?" Her eyes sparkled with an almost manic glee as she bounced on the spot, her voice rising and falling in a singsong pattern. "I don't see a car, so I assume you're here for presents?"

"Hi," Holly said. "Yes, we're just looking to buy a little gift for each other. It's supposed to be a surprise, though, so we'll just browse independently."

"Of course. Let me know if you have any questions and meanwhile..." Millie rushed over with a tray of fudge. "Please enjoy a homemade treat."

"Thank you, that's so sweet." Mack picked up a piece and moaned as she bit into it. "It's delicious. Do you sell this? I wouldn't mind taking some back."

"Oh, yes. It's a Mistletoe family recipe." Millie pointed to the counter where various types of fudge were displayed under a glass case. "I've got traditional chocolate, peppermint swirl, and maple bacon. Come here and have a taste. You have to try them all before you decide."

While Mack followed Millie, Holly eyed the shelves that groaned under the weight of countless knickknacks, ranging from the typical to the bizarre. Among the usual baubles and stars were ornaments shaped like pickles, sushi rolls, and what appeared to be a miniature replica of the gas station itself, complete with tiny blinking lights.

She'd expected gas station staples like snacks and car accessories, but they were vastly outnumbered by an eclectic array of gifts and souvenirs. There was a section dedicated to novelty mugs. "Live, Laugh, Lutefisk" proclaimed one, while another said, "I survived winter in Watertown and all I got was this lousy mug (and frostbite)." A rack of T-shirts bearing slogans like "I'm not yelling, I'm South Dakotan" and "Corn is life" made her chuckle, and she browsed through them, wondering if Mack would like one.

In the background, she heard Mack and Millie discuss the fudge, and she found herself tuning out the chatter, her attention drawn instead to Mack's animated gestures as she spoke. There was something captivating about the way she engaged with people, her genuine interest and quick wit evident even in casual conversation. Holly noticed the way her teal hair that stuck out from underneath her beanie caught the light, how she absentmindedly tucked it behind her ear, and how her infectious smile lit up her whole face.

As she contemplated potential gifts, Holly realized she was subconsciously looking for something that would make Mack laugh, wanting to see that spark of amusement light up her eyes again. She caught herself and shook her head slightly. She had a little crush; there was no point denying that.

Holly was examining a beanie when Mack's voice whispered, "Find anything good?" her breath warm against Holly's ear.

Holly jumped slightly as she turned around and quickly hid the beanie behind her back. "Maybe. But it's a surprise," she stammered, a little flustered by how close they were standing. She gestured to the bag of fudge Mack was holding. "Is that my present?"

"What? No," Mack laughed, shaking her head. "Your present is a surprise too. But," she added, her voice dropping, "I'm always happy to share my fudge with a beautiful woman."

Before Holly could process the flirty comment, Mack was already reaching into the bag. She pulled out a piece of fudge and bit off half. Then, with a mischievous glint in her eye, she held out the other half to Holly.

Holly hesitated for a split second, her heart racing. There was something undeniably intimate about the gesture. She leaned forward, parting her lips slightly as Mack gently placed the fudge in her mouth.

The sweetness of the chocolate exploded on her tongue, and her breath caught in her throat at Mack's fingers brushing against her lips.

"Good?" Mack asked, her voice low and slightly husky.

Holly nodded, not trusting herself to speak. She was acutely aware of Mack's eyes on her lips and wondered what it would be like to close the distance between them, to kiss her... She quickly looked away, her cheeks warming. "It's delicious," she said, clearing her throat. "But I need you to step away now, or your gift won't be a surprise."

"Oh, of course." Mack grinned, and if Holly wasn't mistaken, she was blushing too. "I'll keep myself busy in the next aisle."

Mistletoe Motel

Again, Millie's cheerful voice cut through their conversation. "Finding everything okay, ladies? I forgot to mention, we also sell mystery gift bags over there."

Holly stepped back, feeling slightly dazed. "Yes, thank you." She tried to calm her racing heart. What was happening to her? She'd known Mack for less than twenty-four hours, and yet she found herself drawn to her in a way she couldn't explain. "Mystery bags? What are those?"

"Oh, the mystery gift bags are a fantastic bargain! Each one is filled with a random assortment of Watertown treasures. It's extra fun because you never know what you're gifting. Could be anything from a snow globe to a packet of our famous cheese curds!"

Holly nodded politely, thinking to herself that it sounded more like a clever way for Millie to offload old stock that nobody wanted. Still, curiosity got the better of her, and she wandered over to check out the bags anyway.

In the corner, she found a mountain of brightly colored gift bags, each tied with a gaudy bow. A hand-painted sign propped against the pile proclaimed in glittery letters: *MYSTERY BAGS! $10 each or 5 for $15. Warning: May contain traces of Mistletoe magic!*

Holly chuckled and was about to turn away when something caught her eye. Next to the bags was a small rack of beanies, and one in particular stood out. It was black with a touristy slogan embroidered in teal across the front. Without hesitation, she grabbed it, imagining Mack's laughter when she saw it.

"I'll take this one," she whispered as she handed it to Millie.

"Great choice." Millie winked and hid it behind the counter.

"And I'll have one of those mystery bags, because why not?"

"Make that two." With one hand behind her back, hiding Holly's present, Mack grabbed another mystery bag. "Like you said, Millie, it's a bargain. Oh, and do you mind if I use your phone?"

Chapter 11

Mack

Mack fumbled with the key card, her frozen fingers struggling to grip the plastic. The wind howled around them, whipping snow against their faces as they huddled in the doorway of their motel room.

As they stepped inside, shaking off snow and stamping their feet, Mack's jaw dropped. The room had undergone a complete transformation in their absence.

"Oh. My. God," Holly breathed beside her.

Tinsel garlands were wound around the backs of chairs and the bedframe, glittering in the glow of colored lights that had been haphazardly draped across the walls and stuck on with duct tape. The curtain rod was wrapped in a garland of silver and gold, with tiny ornaments dangling precariously. In the corner, a life-sized inflatable Santa grinned at them, his plastic face reflecting the twinkling lights in a way that was slightly unsettling.

"I think the cleaning lady might have gone a bit overboard," Mack said, unable to suppress a laugh.

Holly joined in, her giggles turning into full-blown

laughter as she took in more details. "Look at the nightstands!"

Mack turned to see two small plastic Christmas trees, one perched on either side of the bed, their branches adorned with miniature ornaments and twinkling with built-in lights.

"Why am I not entirely surprised?" Mack shrugged off her coat, hanging it on the back of a chair.

Holly was still chuckling as she removed her own coat. "I feel like we've stepped into some kind of Christmas fever dream. All we need now is—"

She stopped mid-sentence, her eyes widening as she looked up. Mack followed her gaze and felt her breath catch in her throat. There, dangling from the ceiling directly above them, was a sprig of mistletoe. "Oh...wow. Okay."

Their eyes met, and Mack felt the atmosphere in the room shift. Holly's cheeks were flushed, whether from the cold or something else, Mack couldn't be sure. But the way Holly was looking at her, with a mixture of nervousness and something that looked a lot like desire, made her heart race.

"Well...I guess the Mistletoes really commit to their name," she said with a goofy grin.

"Yeah..." Holly's eyes never left Mack's.

They stood there for a moment, neither moving, the silence stretching between them thick with unspoken thoughts. Mack found herself hyperaware of every detail—the way Holly bit her lip, the soft rise and fall of her chest as she breathed, the faint scent of her perfume mingling with the crisp winter air that clung to their clothes...

The playful glint in Holly's eyes sent a surge of warmth through her, cutting through the lingering chill from outside. Holly's lips curved into a hesitant smile, the kind that felt like an invitation but with just enough uncertainty to make Mack second-guess everything. The air between them grew thick, almost palpable, as if even the garish decorations had fallen still, waiting. Her heart hammered against her ribcage, each beat louder than the last, but she forced herself to speak.

"Do you think it's bad luck if we ignore it?"

"Let's not risk it." Holly swallowed hard. "I mean, it is tradition, right?"

Mack took a small step closer to Holly and reached out, giving her plenty of time to pull away if she wanted to. But Holly didn't move, and Mack gently cupped her cheek and stroked it with her thumb. Her skin was cool from the outdoors, but she could feel the warmth beneath, the faint shiver when Holly's eyelashes fluttered at her touch.

Holly's lips parted just enough to make Mack's knees weak, and that single, silent plea in her gaze was all Mack needed. She leaned in, slowly, and stayed perfectly still, Holly's breath warm and shallow against her lips as they hovered just a heartbeat away.

When Mack finally closed the gap, their lips met softly, but the impact was anything but gentle. Holly's lips were soft, yielding, and she tasted faintly sweet, like the remnants of the chocolate fudge they'd shared earlier. But it was the way Holly responded that made her dizzy. Holly's arms wrapped around her, pulling her closer, deeper, until there was no space left between them, just the heat of their bodies and the intoxicating sensation of lips against lips.

Mack's hand slid to the back of Holly's neck, her fingers tangling in her hair as she tilted her head, deepening the kiss. She could feel Holly's breath hitch, the way her body pressed closer, melting into her like she'd been waiting for this just as much.

Time seemed to blur, the world outside falling away

until all Mack could focus on was the heat of Holly's mouth, the way her breath mingled with hers, the soft, needy sound Holly made in the back of her throat. If there ever was a perfect kiss, this was it.

When they finally pulled apart, their foreheads resting together, Mack's breath came in ragged, shallow bursts. Holly's eyes fluttered open, and the look in them—soft, vulnerable, but laced with that same raw desire—made Mack's heart stutter.

"Merry Christmas," Holly whispered, her lips curving into the smallest, breathless smile.

Mack could only nod, still trying to catch her breath, her fingers still tangled in Holly's hair. She wanted nothing more than to lean in for another kiss, to lose herself in Holly's embrace. But before she could act on that desire, a sharp knock at the door jolted them apart. She let out a frustrated sigh and glanced at Holly, who looked equally flustered, her cheeks flushed and her lips slightly swollen.

"I should...probably get that," Mack said, her voice husky. She took a deep breath, trying to compose herself before opening the door. On the other side stood Maude, balancing a tray with two steaming mugs.

"Merry Christmas Eve, girls!" Maude chirped. "I thought you might like some mulled wine to start off the festivities," she added and stepped into the room without waiting for permission. She paused, glancing around with obvious delight. "Oh my, Darla's done a wonderful job in here, hasn't she?" Then her eyes drifted upward, catching sight of the mistletoe, and a knowing smile spread across her face as she looked between Mack and Holly.

Mack felt her face grow hot. "Thank you for the mulled wine," she said quickly, hoping to change the subject. "That's very thoughtful of you."

"Oh, it's my pleasure, dear." Maude set the tray down on the small table. "I saw the lights were on, so I thought I'd best catch you before you're off again. You two enjoy now." With a final wink, she bustled out, leaving Mack and Holly alone once again.

An awkward silence fell over the room. The kiss still lingered between them, unspoken but impossible to ignore.

Mack cleared her throat, desperate to break the silence. "So," she began, her voice coming out a bit higher than usual as she picked up one of the mugs. "About that romantic Christmas date we planned... Are you still up for it?"

"Of course. I just need to get changed." Holly smiled shyly as she picked up her own mug and took a sip. "Ouch!" She winced and brought a hand to her mouth. "Don't drink it yet. I just burned my lips."

"Are you okay?" Mack asked.

"Yeah." Holly chuckled. "I will be if you kiss them better."

Mack set down her mug and stepped closer, her eyes locked on Holly's lips. "Well, we can't have you injured before our big date," she murmured, her voice low and teasing. She leaned in, brushing her lips softly against Holly's before claiming her mouth.

Mack moaned as Holly's hand slid into her coat and underneath her sweater, teasing her skin and leaving a trail of fire everywhere she touched her.

Mack slid her hand down Holly's side, resting on the curve of her hip. Holly arched into the touch, and a soft whimper escaped her throat.

Their kisses became more urgent, a slow burn igniting into a wildfire, and Mack's senses went into overdrive. The tinny jingle of a tiny ornament falling from the curtain rod, the crinkle of Holly's coat as it slid to the floor, the faint scent of cinnamon from the mulled wine mingling with Holly's perfume—each detail etched itself into her memory.

She smiled into the kiss, overcome by the absurdity and the beauty of their situation. Holly must have felt it too, because she started giggling, the vibrations of her laughter adding a new, delightful dimension to their intimate embrace.

Mack silently thanked her lucky stars for Maude and her mistletoe, grateful for this unexpected bug in her holiday plans that had turned into the most delightful feature. As she pulled back, she saw Holly's eyes were still closed, a contented smile playing on her lips. "Better?"

"Much better," Holly whispered. Her eyes fluttered open, and her smile widened. "But maybe we should make sure. Just to be safe." And with that, she pulled Mack in for another kiss, the mulled wine and their impending date momentarily forgotten.

Chapter 12

Holly

Holly sipped her mulled wine, savoring the warm spices as they danced across her tongue. The Mistletoe Diner buzzed with festive energy around her, but her focus remained on Mack, who sat across the table, phone in hand. The soft glow from the screen illuminated Mack's face as she video-called her sister. She was wearing jeans and a black cashmere sweater and she looked so attractive Holly couldn't keep her eyes off her.

Holly was still buzzing after their make-out session and all she could think of was that she wanted more. So much more. She'd called her parents earlier and could hardly concentrate on the conversation.

"Still no contractions?" Mack asked.

Holly listened intently, picking up the muffled voice on the other end confirming that labor hadn't started yet. She couldn't help but feel a twinge of guilt—part of her was selfishly glad that Mack was still here with her, even as she understood how important it was for Mack to be there for her sister's big moment.

"How are you holding up, Mack?" the voice from the

phone asked, louder this time. "It must be incredibly frustrating being stranded like this."

Mack's eyes flicked up, meeting Holly's gaze. A small smile played at the corners of her mouth. "You know what? Being stranded isn't so bad after all," she replied, her tone light. "As long as the baby waits until I can get there, I'm doing just fine."

Holly grinned sheepishly. The way Mack looked at her, with that mixture of mischief and affection, made her weak in every limb. It was hard to believe that just yesterday, they'd been strangers arguing at an airport. Now, here they were, sharing secret smiles in a kitschy diner, their legs tangled together underneath the table.

"Oh, really?" Mack's sister's voice held a note of curiosity. "Please explain because we were all feeling sorry for you."

Mack's grin widened. "Well, I've made a new friend. Want to meet her?" Without waiting for a response, Mack turned the phone around. "Mom, Dad, Sis—this is Holly. She's stranded too and we're about to have dinner together."

Caught off guard, Holly quickly swallowed her mouthful of wine and waved at the screen. "Hi there," she said, hoping her voice didn't betray her nervousness. "It's nice to meet you all."

Three smiling faces peered back at her from the phone screen. Mack's sister—heavily pregnant and glowing—sat in the center of a big white couch, flanked by an older couple Holly assumed were Mack's parents. The family resemblance was striking; they all shared Mack's warm, expressive eyes, but none of them had brightly colored hair or looked eccentric in any way.

"Holly!" Mack's sister exclaimed. "So you're the reason

my sister isn't chomping at the bit to get home. I'm Sarah, by the way. That's Mom and Dad."

"It's a pleasure to meet you, Holly," Mack's mother chimed in, her smile warm and welcoming. "I hope you're both staying safe in that storm."

Holly nodded, feeling a bit overwhelmed by the sudden introduction. "We're doing our best," she assured them. "The people here in Watertown have been incredibly kind. I'm sure Mack will tell you all about it when she finally makes it home. The storm has died down a bit, so we're hoping we might be able to get a car or a flight tomorrow."

The family on the other end of the call mumbled their hopeful agreement, and Mack got up to sit next to Holly.

As Holly watched Mack interact with her family, she felt a pang of longing. She thought of her own parents, waiting for her in Minneapolis. Would they ever accept her the way Mack's family seemed to embrace Mack? She pushed the thought aside, not wanting to dwell on it in this moment of joy.

"So, Holly," Sarah's voice brought her attention back to the conversation. "What do you do when you're not getting stranded in charming small towns with strange women?"

Holly laughed. "I'm a corporate lawyer, actually. Mergers and acquisitions, mostly."

"Ooh, sounds fancy," Sarah teased. "Mack, you better watch out. Sounds like you've found yourself a real catch."

"Oh, we're not..." Mack chuckled nervously. "It's not what you think, it's... I mean..."

Holly felt her cheeks warm, and she noticed a faint blush creeping up Mack's neck as well as she tried to scramble her way out of the situation. "We're just friends," she lied, backing up Mack. Whatever was happening between them, it was way too soon to discuss with outsiders.

"Sure. Of course." Mack's sister shot them a teasing smile. Well, enjoy your dinner, ladies. I've got a sudden craving for pizza, so I might order us a few. Mack, keep us posted if anything changes with your travel situation, okay?"

"Will do," Mack promised. "And you let me know the second anything starts happening with that baby, got it?"

After a round of goodbyes, Mack ended the call and returned to her seat across the table. She leaned back in her chair as she looked at Holly.

"So, that's my family. I'm sorry they drew conclusions. I didn't know what to say."

"That's okay. They seem wonderful," Holly said honestly. "Very warm and sweet. You're lucky to have them."

"I am," Mack agreed. "I know not everyone has it so easy when it comes to family."

The unspoken reference to Holly's own family situation hung in the air between them. Holly appreciated that Mack didn't push the subject but simply gave her hand a gentle squeeze.

"What about the father of the baby? I noticed there was no man there."

"The father's not in the picture." Mack shrugged. "Sarah went to Cabo with friends for a vacation and a few weeks later she found out she was pregnant. It was a drunken encounter. He wasn't exactly the love of her life. She didn't even remember his last name, but after coming down from the initial shock, she decided to raise the baby by herself." Her thumb traced lazy circles on the back of Holly's hand, sending shivers up her arm.

"That's so brave of her."

"You know what? I think it will be good for her. I think the baby will give her the sense of purpose in life she's been looking for. Sarah's always been the wild child in the family," Mack said. "She dropped out of school, and she had several jobs before she finally found one she liked, working at an animal shelter. Her relationships have been tumultuous—she tends to go for the bad boys, and it never ends well. But this pregnancy... It's like it's given her a new focus. I've never seen her so determined and excited about anything before."

Holly smiled. "Sometimes the unexpected things in life end up being exactly what we need," she mused, her eyes meeting Mack's. The double meaning wasn't lost on either of them.

"Speaking of unexpected..." Mack lowered her voice as she leaned in closer. "I can't stop thinking about earlier. In our room."

"Me neither," Holly admitted. "I know we should probably talk about...whatever this is between us. But right now, all I can think about is kissing you again and ..." She looked down at the placemat in front of her, studying the slogan. *Mistletoe Diner: Where Strangers Become Friends and Friends Become Family.* She wasn't sure what she was trying to say; the past twenty-four hours had been a whirlwind. "Well," she finally continued, "I guess I'm thinking about the fact that we'll be sharing a bed again tonight."

Mack's eyes darkened, and Holly watched as she swallowed hard. But before she could respond, Marty appeared at their table, his Santa hat slightly askew and his cheeks rosy with holiday cheer. "Ho-ho-ho!" he boomed, setting down two plates. "Here's your starter, ladies! Corn fritters and cheese curds—battered and deep-fried, served with ranch dressing."

The moment broken, Holly and Mack leaned back, both a little flustered.

"This looks...amazing, Marty," Holly managed, trying to regain her composure. "Thank you."

"My pleasure!" Marty beamed. "And don't forget, leave some room for the famous Mistletoe turkey and dessert!"

Mack chuckled, picking up her fork. "Well, let's try this. It would be a shame to let Marty's famous food go to waste." She speared a piece of cheese curd and held it out for Holly to try.

Holly bit into it, enjoying the crispy exterior and gooey center. With Mack's smile filling her heart and the taste of fried cheese on her tongue, she savored an even sweeter taste—a hint of new beginnings, wrapped in tinsel and served with a side of serendipity.

Chapter 13

Mack

Mack leaned back in the booth, pleasantly full from the main course. Marty's famous Mistletoe turkey had lived up to its reputation —juicy, perfectly seasoned, and served with all the trimmings. The festive atmosphere of the diner, combined with Holly's company, had made for an unforgettable Christmas Eve dinner.

When their table was cleared, she saw an opportunity. With a dramatic flourish, she reached into her satchel and pulled out two items—a small, neatly wrapped present and the by-now crumpled mystery paper bag from Millie's gas station. She placed them on the table with a grin.

"Ta-da!" she announced. "I believe it's time for our gift exchange, princess."

Holly's eyebrows shot up. "Well, well," she said, and with a chuckle, she mirrored Mack's actions, producing her own wrapped gift and mystery bag from her purse.

"So, who goes first?"

"You go," Holly said, practically bouncing in her seat with excitement.

Mack didn't need to be told twice. She grabbed the wrapped gift, tearing into it with childlike enthusiasm. As the paper fell away, she burst into laughter. In her hands was a black beanie with teal letters embroidered across the front: *Watertown: Our Departures are as Rare as a Warm Winter Day!*

"Oh my god," she wheezed between fits of laughter. "This is perfect! She immediately pulled the beanie on, adjusting it so her teal hair peeked out from underneath. "How do I look?"

"Like a true Watertown tourist. It suits you."

"Maybe I'll model it for you later," Mack said suggestively. "Seriously, though. I love it. Thank you, Holly. This is going to be a great reminder. Not that I'd ever forget," she quickly added. "The past two days with you have been the best surprise."

"Likewise." Holly took her hand and squeezed it. "I won't forget either."

Mack squeezed her back and felt a little emotional because truthfully, she didn't want to part ways. Not wanting to come across as dramatic, though, she plastered on a grin and turned to her mystery bag. "Now...what have we got here?" She opened it, peered inside, and pulled out the first item. "Oh wow. This is...something else." It was a small wooden plaque bearing the words *Watertown Winter Wonderland* 2017.

"Nice. Seven-year-old stock." Holly laughed. "I don't even want to know what else is in there."

"Well, I'm about to show you anyway," Mack said, pulling out a key chain with a faded *I love Watertown* logo, a pair of novelty sunglasses shaped like snowflakes, and a small bag of "Mistletoe Mint" hard candies. She chuckled, displaying her haul. She put on the sunglasses and held up the key chain. "I don't know about you, but I think I've found my new signature look."

Holly laughed. "Oh yes, very chic. That bag was definitely a winner." When Mack gestured to her presents, she opened the first one, revealing a coffee mug with *I Object to Mornings* printed on it in bold, playful letters. She burst into laughter, turning the mug in her hands to admire it from all angles.

"Oh, Mack, I love it! I'll be thinking of you every morning when I have my coffee now."

Mack's eyes met Holly's. "You could always call me when you're thinking of me," she teased, her voice low and playful.

Holly bit her lip, a mischievous glint in her eye. "Or maybe we could meet up? We do live in the same city, after all."

"We should." Mack hesitated for a moment, then asked, "Actually, when we're back...can I take you out on a real date?" Her leg brushed against Holly's under the table, and she placed a hand on Holly's thigh. They were back sitting next to each other, leaning in closer as the evening progressed.

Holly's breath hitched slightly at the contact. "I'd love that," she murmured, her eyes flickering to Mack's lips before meeting her gaze again.

Mack's hand found Holly's under the table, their fingers intertwining. "I can think of a few places I'd love to take you."

A charged silence fell between them, a moment that seemed to stretch on forever, and Mack was dying to know what went through her mind. "I suppose I should open my mystery bag now," she finally said as she reached for it. "Let's see what Millie's clearance bin had in store for me."

Holly pulled out the first item—a slightly dented can of non-alcoholic Watertown Winter Ale, followed by a key chain with a small plastic sprig of mistletoe attached. "Aww...How fitting," she mused, dangling the key chain above them.

Mack's cheeks warmed at the memory of their kiss under the mistletoe. "I wouldn't mind a repeat performance."

"Me either." Holly shot her a flirty look and held her gaze for a beat before she pulled the third item out of the mystery bag. It was a pocket-sized booklet titled *101 Fun Facts About Watertown*. "This looks...informative." She chuckled, flipping through the pages. "Did you know that Watertown is home to the world's largest pheasant statue?"

"I did not know that." Mack raised a brow. "Perhaps we should add that to our list of things to do before we leave."

Holly licked her lips and smiled. "I think we can put our time to better use, don't you?"

Mack's stomach did a flip as she shifted even closer. They were definitely still on the same page and she couldn't wait to have Holly to herself tonight. "What did you have in mind?"

"I don't know...maybe some exploration of the more personal kind?"

Mack brought her lips to Holly's ear, her voice dropping to a husky whisper. "Personal exploration, huh? I like the sound of that."

Holly's eyes sparkled with mischief as she traced her finger along Mack's arm. "I was hoping you would. Any particular areas you'd like to...explore?"

"Oh, I have a few ideas," Mack replied, her gaze trailing down Holly's body before meeting her eyes again. "But I'm open to suggestions."

Holly bit her lip, suppressing a grin. "Well, I've always been curious about the local...scenery. Especially the hidden gems."

"I'd be happy to give you a thorough tour. Though it might take all night."

"All night?" Holly echoed. "Promise?"

Mack was about to respond when a loud crash from the kitchen made them both jump. They turned to see Marty emerge from the kitchen, a cloud of powdered sugar billowing around him like a sweet, festive fog. His Christmas sweater was a canvas of white splotches, and a streak of what looked like apple filling decorated his left cheek.

He adjusted his now even more lopsided Santa hat, leaving a sugar handprint on his forehead, and brushed ineffectually at his clothes, sending another puff of sugar into the air. Oblivious to the amused stares of the diners, he straightened his posture and put on his best jolly expression, ready to make his dessert announcement.

"Ho-ho-ho!" he bellowed. "Who's ready for the Mistletoe Diner's famous Christmas apple pie?" He paused, noticing the patrons' startled expressions. "Oh, don't mind me. Just had a little tussle with the dessert trolley. Now, are you up for something sweet?"

Mack and Holly exchanged glances, barely suppressing their laughter. The moment had been broken, but the promise of what could be lingered between them. As Marty bustled toward a neighboring table, Mack put an arm around Holly's shoulders and whispered, "To be continued?"

Chapter 14

Holly

Holly shrugged off her coat as they entered the motel room, the warmth enveloping her after the chilly night air.

Her skin tingled with anticipation, her mind buzzing from the effects of wine and the intoxicating tension that had been building between them all evening. The playful banter, the lingering touches, the heated glances across the dinner table—it all culminated in a delicious, almost unbearable anticipation. Holly's nerves were on edge, every sense heightened. She could still feel the phantom touch of Mack's hand on her thigh under the table, could still see the mischievous glint in her eyes as they'd made thinly veiled innuendos. The flirting had been relentless, each exchange adding fuel to a smoldering fire that now threatened to consume her.

Before she could hang up her coat, Mack took it from her hands and tossed it unceremoniously to the floor along with her own.

"Priorities," she murmured with a mischievous smile.

Holly barely had a chance to register the movement

before Mack's lips were on hers—desperate, hungry, as though she had been waiting for this all night. Holly gasped into the kiss, caught between surprise and the rapid escalation of desire that surged through her. Their lips crashed with a fierce urgency, and Mack's hands cupped her face, fingers tangling in her hair as she gently pushed her against the wall. She was in-charge and Holly loved it, her body responding instinctively, grinding into Mack's.

Her arms wrapped around Mack's waist, pulling her against her, deepening the kiss while Mack's hands roamed restlessly, tracing the curve of Holly's neck, skimming down her sides.

Holly was drowning in the kiss—Mack's lips, her hands, the way her body pressed insistently against hers. There was a desperation in Mack's touch, something almost primal. Their breaths mingled, short and ragged, between fevered kisses, and Holly felt her pulse quickening, her heart beating wildly against her ribs. Mack's hand found its way underneath Holly's sweater, tracing her back and making Holly shiver with anticipation. Her touch was electric, and Holly had never felt so present, so aware of her own body, of every inch of her that brushed against Mack's.

Small, needy sounds escaped from Holly's throat as Mack's mouth moved to her jawline, trailing hot, open-mouthed kisses along her skin. Her knees felt weak, but Mack's hands were there, holding her up, steadying her against the wall. Her thoughts were a chaotic whirl—flashes of longing, of the undeniable attraction she'd felt for the past twenty-four hours.

Mack's hands roamed over her back, her fingers digging into her skin before they lowered to her behind and squeezed it. She pulled back slightly, just enough to look into Holly's eyes, her breath coming in short, shallow gasps.

Her blue eyes were dark, filled with the same need, the same intensity that coursed through Holly's veins. For a moment, they stood there, breathing each other in, their foreheads pressed together, sharing the silence, the rawness of the moment.

Holly's heart was racing, her skin flushed and hot. She felt dizzy, intoxicated and yet so present, alive in a way she hadn't felt in a long time. She was caught between wanting to savor every second and the overwhelming desire to let go completely.

"You know..." Mack's voice was barely a whisper, her words rough and breathless as she brushed a thumb across Holly's cheek. "I've wanted to do that all night."

Holly's lips tugged into a smile, still tingling from the searing kiss. "Me too," she whispered. "I want you. I want all of you." Tugging at Mack's sweater, she waited for her to raise her arms so she could pull it off, along with her T-shirt.

Holly's breath hitched as Mack stood before her, stripped down to nothing but her sports bra and jeans. The soft, dim light of the motel room illuminated her toned arms and shoulders, revealing the lean, defined muscles that flexed with every subtle movement. Holly's eyes trailed over Mack's body, tracing the delicate contours of her collarbone, the curve of her biceps, and the smooth expanse of her abdomen, only partially obscured by the hem of the snug sports bra.

She was mesmerized by the faint rise and fall of Mack's chest as she breathed, her heartbeat still rapid from the intensity of their kiss. The sight of her like this, raw and vulnerable yet utterly confident, made Holly want to devour her. She was desperate to touch her everywhere, to feel the warmth of her skin beneath her fingertips, to explore every inch of her.

Her gaze traveled upward, lingering on the swell of Mack's breasts before meeting her gaze again. Mack's eyes held her captive—their usual mischievous glint now replaced with something deeper, something more intense as she removed her sports bra and dropped it to the floor.

Mack's breasts were small and firm, yet undeniably sensual, her skin smooth and pale, with faint traces of freckles across her chest that Holly hadn't noticed before. Her nipples were hard, a soft blush of pink that contrasted with the ivory of her skin.

Holly felt the heat radiating from her, the barely restrained power in the way she held herself. Her hands trembled slightly as she reached for the hem of her own sweater, pulling it over her head in one swift motion. She stood before Mack in her lace bra, the delicate fabric hugging her form and exposing just enough to make her feel both bold and vulnerable at once. Her skin prickled with anticipation, goose bumps rising along her arms, and she could feel Mack's gaze on her, burning into her skin.

For a moment, neither of them moved, the air between them crackling with tension. Holly's breath came shallow and fast as she teetered on the edge of restraint and desire. Every nerve in her body was alight with sensation, every inch of her aching for Mack's touch.

Mack reached out, her fingers grazing Holly's arm lightly, as if testing the boundaries of her self-control, and Holly instinctively leaned into it, craving more.

"You're so beautiful," she murmured as she slid Holly's bra straps over her shoulders. She wrapped her arms around Holly to unclip it and leaned into her, brushing her mouth against Holly's. "Come here."

Her lips parted as she slid her tongue over Holly's upper lip, a low hum escaping her throat. Holly felt the world tilt, heat flooding every inch of her skin as they fell into a passionate kiss, their tongues dancing together. She wrapped her arms around Mack's neck and sighed at the delicious sensation of skin against skin.

Mack's hands cupped Holly's breasts, her thumbs brushing over her already sensitive nipples, sending a wave of pleasure coursing through her body. She arched into the touch, her hands finding their way over Mack's shoulders and her back. And then Mack's mouth was on her breasts, kissing them, sucking and biting her nipples.

Holly moaned, her hips rocking against Mack's thigh. Heat pooled between her legs, the ache building inside her.

Mack pulled her away from the wall, guiding her toward the bed with a sense of urgency, her lips never leaving Holly's skin. They stumbled together, falling onto the bed in a tangle of limbs, and Holly laughed softly, the sound cut off by another kiss. Mack's weight settled over her, their bodies perfectly aligned as Mack's thigh pressed between Holly's legs, hard and insistent.

Mack's lips found Holly's neck again, her hands sliding lower, tugging at the waistband of Holly's jeans, her fingers deft and practiced as she unbuttoned them and slid them down her legs. Holly kicked them off, her body humming with anticipation as Mack's hands returned, this time slipping beneath the waistband of her underwear, teasing her in a way that made her gasp, her back arching off the bed.

"God, Holly," Mack whispered against her skin, her voice husky and raw. "You have no idea how much I've been fantasizing about this."

Holly barely had time to respond before Mack's fingers slid lower, finding the heat between her legs. She was so wet, her body aching for more, and when Mack's fingers began to move in slow, steady circles, Holly's moan was low and needy, her fingers gripping the sheets beneath her.

"What do you want, Holly?"

Holly couldn't think, couldn't find words, so in answer, she poured everything she felt into a kiss, wrapping her arms around Mack and pulling her tightly against her.

Mack continued her slow, torturous rhythm, driving her closer and closer to the edge with every stroke. Holly's mind was a haze of pleasure, her hips moving in time with Mack's hand as she unraveled beneath her.

Mack's lips were everywhere—on her neck, her collarbone, trailing soft, biting kisses down the slope of her breast, her tongue flicking teasingly across her nipple before pulling it into her mouth. Holly gasped at the sensation, her body arching into Mack's touch, her fingers tangled in Mack's hair as she held her there, not wanting to let go, not wanting the moment to end. The warmth of Mack's mouth, her hands, the slick heat between them—it was all too much and yet never enough.

The tension coiled tight in her belly, her hips moving instinctively, chasing the pleasure that pulsed between her legs, the sensation of Mack's fingers driving her mad. Lost in the rhythm of her body, the heat and pressure were building inside her like a storm on the verge of breaking.

"Mack," Holly moaned, her voice barely a whisper, breathless and desperate, her body trembling with need. "Yes..." She opened her eyes, finding Mack staring back at her, her gaze dark and intense, filled with the same desire that flooded Holly's veins.

"What do you want?" Mack asked again, her voice rough with need, her fingers never stopping, their rhythm steady, maddeningly slow. She pressed her forehead against

Holly's, their breaths mingling in the charged air between them.

"I want to feel you inside me," Holly whispered through quick breaths.

Mack groaned against her mouth as she kissed her, and Holly could feel the tension in Mack's body too, the way she trembled against her, barely holding herself back. Mack carefully pushed two fingers inside her and Holly gasped, hanging on the edge of release.

She broke the kiss, her head falling back against the pillow as her breath came in ragged gasps, her eyes fluttering shut. Mack pressed her lips to Holly's throat, and even as her body surged with pleasure, Holly's hands roamed over Mack's back, her nails digging in, urging her on, needing more, needing everything.

"Please..." She bucked her hips against Mack's hand, her body trembling with the force of her climax. Her pleasure coiled tighter and tighter until everything inside her shattered, her moans loud and unabashed as she gave herself over completely to the moment.

Mack's hand never faltered, drawing out every last bit of pleasure until Holly was a trembling mess beneath her. She held her close, their bodies tangled together, her kisses softening into something more tender, more intimate.

For a few blissful moments, they lay together, intertwined, their breaths slowly evening out as the heat of the moment began to dissipate. Holly's heart was still racing, her skin flushed and tingling from the aftershocks of her release.

Mack smiled, pressing a soft kiss to her skin before pulling back just enough to look into her eyes. Holly's heart swelled at the sight of her, her hair tousled, her eyes heavy-lidded with affection and a cute hint of smugness. She looked beautiful.

"Are you okay?" Mack whispered, her voice gentle.

Holly nodded, reaching up to tuck a stray strand of Mack's hair behind her ear. "That was amazing." She shot her a wicked smile as she shifted, rolling them over so she straddled Mack. Her fingers traced slow, teasing circles on Mack's bare skin, and leaning down, she kissed her softly before pulling back to whisper against her lips, "Now it's my turn to make you beg."

Chapter 15

Mack

The insistent knocking pulled Mack from a deep, contented sleep. She groaned, burying her face deeper into the pillow, hoping whoever it was would give up and go away. But the knocking continued, growing more urgent with each passing second.

Mack cracked open an eye, squinting against the pale morning light filtering through the thin motel curtains. For a moment, she was disoriented, the unfamiliar room coming into focus slowly. Then the events of the previous night came flooding back, and a slow smile spread across her face.

She turned her head to find Holly still fast asleep beside her, her dark hair fanned out on the pillow, her bare shoulders peeking out from under the covers. Mack's heart swelled at the sight, a mix of tenderness and desire washing over her. She wanted nothing more than to curl up closer to Holly, to trace the curve of her shoulder with her fingertips, to wake her with soft kisses. But the persistent knocking shattered that dream.

"Coming, coming," Mack grumbled under her breath, careful not to wake Holly as she slid out of bed. The cool air hit her bare skin, raising goose bumps, and she shivered. Glancing around the room, she spotted her clothes strewn haphazardly across the floor.

She quickly pulled on her jeans and sweater, running a hand through her tousled hair in a futile attempt to make it somewhat presentable. As she padded toward the door, she caught sight of herself in the mirror and had to stifle a laugh. Her hair was a wild mess, her sweater was inside out, and there was a distinct purple mark on her neck that hadn't been there the night before. She looked thoroughly disheveled, but there wasn't time to do anything about it now.

The knocking came again, more insistent this time. "I'm coming, I'm coming," Mack called out, her voice still rough with sleep. She glanced back at Holly, making sure the noise hadn't woken her, before opening the door.

"Look, we don't need a wake-up call. It's Christmas morning, the car rentals aren't even open ye—" Mack's words died on her lips as she found herself face-to-face with two strangers. They weren't Maude or any of her team she'd come to expect. Instead, a middle-aged couple stood before her, looking just as confused as she felt.

The woman, petite with graying hair and kind eyes, spoke first. "Oh, I'm so sorry," she said, her voice tinged with embarrassment. "We must have the wrong room. We're looking for our daughter, Holly. The receptionist said she was in Room Fifteen, but..." She trailed off, her eyes taking in Mack's disheveled appearance with growing uncertainty.

Mack's brain, still foggy with sleep, took a moment to process the information. Then it hit her like a bucket of ice water. These weren't just any strangers—they were Holly's

Mistletoe Motel

parents. The parents Holly had been so nervous about reconciling with. The parents who would be shocked if they knew their daughter was sharing a bed with her. But she couldn't lie to them, could she? They'd driven all the way here from Minneapolis and must have left in the middle of the night.

"Um, no, you've got the right room," Mack finally said, her mind racing. "Holly is here. She's just...still asleep. There were no more rooms left, and she kindly offered to share her room with me," she added, hoping that would look better to them. "If you could give me a minute to wake her up?"

The couple exchanged a look that Mack couldn't quite decipher. The man, tall and distinguished-looking with salt-and-pepper hair, nodded stiffly. "Of course," he said, his tone polite but cool. "We'll wait out here."

Mack nodded, closing the door perhaps a bit too quickly. She leaned against it for a moment, her heart pounding. This was not how she had envisioned starting Christmas morning.

Taking a deep breath, she crossed the room to Holly's side of the bed. Holly was still sound asleep, oblivious to the chaos that was about to unfold. Mack hated to wake her, especially like this, but there was no avoiding it.

"Holly," Mack said softly, gently shaking her shoulder. "Holly, wake up. We've got company."

Holly stirred, mumbling something incoherent before burrowing deeper into the covers. Under different circumstances, Mack would have found it adorable. Now, it just added to her growing anxiety.

"Holly, seriously, you need to wake up," she said, her voice more urgent this time. "Your parents are here."

That did it. Holly's eyes flew open, wide with shock.

"What?" she gasped, sitting up so quickly she nearly head-butted Mack. "My parents? Here? Now?"

Mack nodded, stepping back to give Holly space. "They're waiting outside. I told them I'd wake you up."

"Oh my god," Holly groaned, burying her face in her hands. "Oh my god, oh my god. This can't be happening." Then she scrambled out of bed, nearly tripping over the tangled sheets in her haste. She darted around the room, snatching up pieces of clothing and pulling them on haphazardly.

"Where's my bra?" she asked, her voice edging on panic as she lifted pillows and peered under the bed. "And my sweater?"

Despite the gravity of the situation, Mack couldn't help but smile at Holly's frantic search. She spotted the missing bra hanging from the bedside lamp—how it got there, she couldn't quite remember—and handed it to Holly. "Here," she said. "And your sweater is...ah, over there, by the inflatable Santa."

Holly snatched the items, muttering a quick thanks as she continued to dress. Mack watched her for a moment, wishing she could do something to ease Holly's obvious distress. "Hey," she said softly. "It's going to be okay. Take a deep breath."

Holly paused, meeting Mack's eyes. For a moment, the panic in her gaze softened, replaced by something warmer. "Thank you," she said. "How do I look?"

Mack stepped closer, gently smoothing Holly's hair. "You look beautiful," she said. "Are you ready for this? I told them you were kind enough to share your room with me, so they might not think anything of it. I mean, of you and me together..."

"Oh, they will. They'll know." Holly took a deep, shaky

breath. "But that's the whole point, right? That I need them to accept who I am." She moved toward the door, pausing with her hand on the handle. She looked back at Mack, a question in her eyes. "Should you... I mean, do you want to..."

Mack understood the unspoken question. "How about I get us coffees while you catch up with your parents?" she suggested. "Do they like cappuccino?"

"Yes, they do. Thank you so much." Holly waited until Mack had put on her boots and coat and stopped her before she was about to head out. "Wait..." She kissed her softly, lingering for just a moment. "Thank you for last night."

"No, thank *you*." Mack squeezed her hand, opened the door, and slipped out, giving Holly's parents a polite nod. She heard greetings behind her; Holly's mom sounded emotional, and Mack had a feeling everything would be okay. Things seemed to have a way of working out lately.

The streets were quiet, most of Watertown still asleep on this Christmas morning. It had stopped snowing—a fresh layer had fallen overnight, transforming the town into a picture-perfect winter wonderland—and the network was back so she was able to check her messages; nothing from her parents or her sister yet.

She was getting home today; she could feel it. Now that the storm had subsided, she'd take anything she could. A flight, a rental car... even a bus. Lost in thought, Mack almost walked right past the Mistletoe Diner. A cheery "Merry Christmas!" from Marty, who was outside, clearing the path to the entrance, snapped her back to reality.

"Merry Christmas, Marty. You're up early."

Marty chuckled. "Christmas waits for no one! Besides, there's breakfast to prepare. Will you and Holly be joining us later?"

"I'm not sure yet. Holly's parents showed up unexpectedly this morning, so I'm just here to grab a few takeout coffees, if that's okay?"

Marty's eyebrows shot up. "Oh my! So, what can I get for you this fine Christmas morning?"

"Four cappuccinos to go, please," Mack said. "And an extra black coffee. I'll have that here while I call my family. And...do you have any apple pie left from last night? Holly really loved it and her parents drove here from Minneapolis. I think they might be hungry."

Marty winked. "For you, I'm sure I can find some leftovers. Come on in, it's cold outside."

Inside the diner, the scent of fresh coffee and baking pastries enveloped Mack. She was the first one in, she noticed, as she sat at the counter, watching Marty and two staff members bustle about.

Mack called her sister, but there was no answer. Then she tried her parents, and again, there was no answer. She was starting to worry until a message from her mother came in. "Sorry dear, we're driving. I'll call you back in twenty minutes."

She frowned. What did that mean? Were they driving to the hospital with her sister? Were they driving to the store because Sarah had cravings again?

"Here you go," Marty said, setting a tray with four large coffees and a paper bag in front of her. "It's on the house—consider it a Christmas gift."

Mack's eyes widened as she looked up from her phone. "Marty, you don't have to—"

"Nonsense," Marty interrupted with a wave of his hand. "It's Christmas, and by the looks of it, you might be able to get home today. One of my waitresses told me they were bringing in extra Greyhounds to leave from the bus station throughout the day for all the stranded tourists. Now go on, before those coffees get cold."

"That's so kind of you. You've all been so kind." She thanked him profusely before heading back out into the cold, carefully balancing the tray of coffees. As she walked, her mind drifted back to her sister and her parents. She would drop off the coffee and the pie, then head to the bus station to see if she could get a ride home. It felt bittersweet having to say goodbye to Holly after such a beautiful time together, especially because it would end so abruptly. She was hopeful they'd see each other again, but for now, Holly needed time with her parents, and Mack needed to be with her family.

Chapter 16

Holly

Holly's heart raced as she opened the door, coming face-to-face with her parents for the first time in nearly a year. The moment felt surreal, like a scene from a movie playing out in slow motion. Her mother's eyes, brimming with tears, met hers, and before Holly could say a word, she was enveloped in a tight embrace.

"Oh, sweetheart," her mother whispered, her voice thick with emotion. "I've missed you so much."

Holly's eyes welled up as she returned the hug, breathing in the familiar scent of her mother. It was a scent that brought back a flood of memories—childhood Christmases, family dinners, quiet conversations over cups of tea. For a moment, she allowed herself to melt into the embrace, to be that little girl again, safe in her mother's arms.

When they pulled apart, Holly turned to her father. He stood a few steps back, his posture stiff, his expression unreadable. He had always been the more reserved of her parents, less prone to emotional displays. But as their eyes met, Holly saw a softening in his gaze.

"Hi, Dad," she said.

He cleared his throat, nodding. "Hello, Holly." There was a pause, and then, in a move that surprised her, he stepped forward and pulled her into a brief, awkward hug. It wasn't much, but coming from her father, it spoke volumes.

"How did you find me?" Holly asked as she ushered them into the room. "I don't remember mentioning the name of the motel on the phone.

"We started driving at three in the morning, as soon as the snow stopped," her mother explained. "We didn't want to wake you up, so we traced the number you'd called us on back to this motel. We wanted to bring you home for Christmas."

Holly's heart swelled at their effort, even as a twinge of panic set in. Her gaze darted around the room, suddenly hyperaware of every detail. The garish decorations seemed even more outlandish in the light of day, and she cringed inwardly as her parents took in the sight.

Her father's eyebrows rose when he saw the modified wall art. "'Don't fall asleep without flossing'?" he read aloud, his tone a mix of confusion and amusement.

"Oh, that," Holly said, feeling her cheeks warm. "It's a long story. The room came with some...interesting decor."

Her mother's gaze traveled upward, and Holly's stomach dropped as she remembered the mistletoe hanging from the ceiling. In her panic to get dressed, she had completely forgotten about it.

"Well," her mother said, a note of forced cheerfulness in her voice, "they certainly went all out with the Christmas spirit, didn't they?"

Holly nodded, grateful for her mother's attempt to gloss

over the awkwardness. She busied herself with making the bed, trying to erase any evidence of the night before. "Please, have a seat," she said, gesturing to the small table by the window. "I'm sorry it's not very comfortable. You must be tired."

As her parents settled into the chairs, Holly caught her mother's gaze lingering on the scattered candles around the room, and Holly felt a flash of defensiveness.

"We tried to make the best of the situation," she said, her voice coming out sharper than she'd intended. She took a deep breath, reminding herself that this was supposed to be about reconciliation. "It wasn't ideal, but Mack and I actually had a nice time."

"Mack?" her father asked, his brow furrowing. "Is that the young woman who answered the door? How do you two know each other?"

Holly perched on the edge of the bed, facing her parents. This was it—the moment of truth. "We were both stranded, and when there was only one room left here, I offered to share it with her."

Her mother cleared her throat. "In one bed? With a stranger?" The question hung in the air, heavy with implication.

Holly felt a surge of frustration. She was tired of hiding, tired of pretending. "Yes, Mom, in one bed," she said firmly. "I'm an adult, and I can make my own decisions."

Her father shifted uncomfortably in his chair but remained silent. Her mother looked like she was about to say something then thought better of it.

"Look," Holly said, "I know this isn't what you expected to find. But I want you to know that I didn't plan any of this. All I wanted was to come home, to see you both. I was hoping we could start with a clean slate, with open communication." She paused, looking from her mother to her father. "I was hoping for some form of acceptance from you. No, I didn't plan to meet Mack or to share a room with her. She wanted to be with her family as much as I wanted to be with you. But at the same time...meeting her has been a blessing. We've had a wonderful time together."

The room fell silent for a moment. Holly's heart pounded as she waited for her parents' reaction. It was her mother who moved first. She stood up, tears glistening in her eyes, and crossed the small space to sit beside Holly on the bed.

"Oh, sweetheart," she whispered. "I want to start over too. I've missed you so much." She wrapped her arm around Holly's shoulders, pulling her close.

Holly leaned into her mother's embrace, allowing herself to hope that maybe, just maybe, things could get better.

Their moment was interrupted by a knock at the door before Mack let herself in. Her arms were laden with a tray of coffees and a paper bag that smelled tantalizingly of cinnamon and apples.

"Sorry to interrupt," she said, her eyes darting nervously between Holly and her parents. "I thought you might all like some coffee and pie."

"That's very thoughtful of you," Holly's mother said, rising from the bed. "You must be Mack."

Mack set the tray and bag on the table. "It's nice to meet you both," she said, offering a tentative smile. "I wasn't sure how you took your coffee, so there's sugar on the side." Her phone rang, and Holly watched as Mack's face went pale, her eyes widening as she listened to the person on the other end. "Okay, I'll try to get there as quickly as I can." The call was brief, and when Mack hung up, she looked shell-shocked.

"Mack?" Holly asked. "What is it? Are you okay?"

Mack blinked, as if coming out of a trance. "That was my mom," she said, her voice barely above a whisper. "Sarah's gone into labor."

"Sarah?" Holly's mother asked, looking between them.

"My sister," Mack explained, her words tumbling out in a rush. "She's pregnant—well, obviously. My parents didn't want to let me know until they were sure. Apparently, there have been three false alarms in the past few days, but...it's really happening now, and—oh my God, I need to pack and get to the bus station. Unless the airport has reopened. Do you know anything about that?"

"We'll drive you. It would be quicker," Holly's father suggested. We're going the same way, and it could take hours before the first flight or bus leaves."

Holly's mother nodded in agreement. "Of course. Please let us take you."

Mack looked stunned. "Are you sure? I don't want to impose..."

"Nonsense," Holly's mother said firmly. "It's Christmas, and family is important. We'll get you to the hospital."

Holly felt a surge of affection for her parents in that moment. Despite their discomfort and the unexpected situation they'd found themselves in, they were reaching out to help a stranger.

"Thank you," Mack said. "I can't tell you how much this means to me." As she began to gather her things, Holly packed her own bag. They moved around each other with a familiarity that belied the short time they'd known each other, and Holly couldn't help but wonder what might have been if circumstances were different.

"I'll just run down to the front desk to check you out," Holly's father said, excusing himself.

Holly zipped her bag closed and stopped him. "No, I'll go. I want to thank the motel owner. Maude's been wonderful, and it wouldn't feel right to leave without saying goodbye."

Chapter 17

Mack

The steady hum of tires on asphalt had become a soothing white noise over the past three hours. Mack sat in the back seat of the Petersons' silver Volvo V90 station wagon, a car that seemed to embody everything she'd imagined about Holly's parents. The leather seats were pristine, not a crumb or stray hair in sight, and the new-car smell still lingered faintly in the air.

Her leg bounced nervously as she stared out the window, watching the snowy landscape rush by. The highway stretched out before them, a ribbon of gray cutting through the white expanse. Occasional clusters of evergreens, their branches heavy with snow, broke up the monotony of the view.

She glanced at her phone for what felt like the hundredth time, willing it to vibrate with another update from her mother. The last message had come through about twenty minutes ago: *Sarah's doing great. Contractions are getting closer together.*

Mack's stomach churned with a mixture of excitement and anxiety. She was going to be an aunt. The reality of it was finally sinking in, along with the growing fear that she might miss the birth despite their best efforts.

"So, Mack," Holly's mother's voice cut through her thoughts as she turned around in the passenger seat once again. "You mentioned earlier that you work in software engineering. What exactly does that entail?"

Mack blinked, pulling her attention away from the window. "Oh, well, I work on developing AI-driven applications. My current project is a personal assistant app that uses machine learning to anticipate users' needs."

"That sounds very...modern," Mrs. Peterson replied, her tone a mix of politeness and bewilderment. "And do you enjoy your work?"

"I do, very much." Mack nodded, trying to keep her answers concise yet polite. She was grateful for the Petersons' kindness in driving her to Minneapolis, but the constant questions were beginning to wear on her already frayed nerves.

"And your family? What do your parents do?" Mrs. Peterson pressed on.

"Mom," Holly interjected from beside Mack, her voice tinged with exasperation. "Maybe we could give Mack a break from the interrogation? Just for now?"

"It's okay, really," Mack said, offering a small smile. "I appreciate your interest, Mrs. Peterson. I'm just grateful you're all willing to help me get to the hospital. And to answer your question—" She stopped herself when her phone buzzed, and her heart leapt as she read the new message from her mother. "Her cervix is fully dilated," she read aloud. "I...I don't even know what that means exactly," she admitted. "I really should have read up on this stuff."

Linda's head whipped around so fast Mack was surprised she didn't get whiplash. "Oh my! That means we need to hurry!" She turned to her husband, her voice rising. "Peter, we need to go faster!"

Mr. Peterson—Peter Peterson—glanced at his wife, his expression a mix of amusement and concern. "Dear, I'm already going five over the speed limit. We'll get there."

"But the baby!" Linda exclaimed, her hands fluttering in the air as if she could somehow will the car to move faster. "Mack's going to miss it!"

Mack felt a surge of anxiety at Linda's words, but before she could spiral into panic mode, she felt Holly's hand slip into hers. The simple gesture grounded her, and she squeezed back gratefully.

"Mom," Holly said. "Please stay calm. Panicking isn't going to get us there any faster."

Linda took a deep breath, visibly trying to compose herself. "You're right, of course. Peter, don't drive faster. Drive safely. We don't want any accidents."

"That was the plan, dear," he said and continued to concentrate on the road.

Linda twisted in her seat to face Mack again, offering what was clearly meant to be an encouraging smile but came across more as a nervous grimace. "Don't worry, Mack. We'll get you there in time. Even the final stage can take hours, especially for first-time mothers."

Her gaze dropped to where Mack's and Holly's hands were intertwined on the seat between them. Mack hadn't even realized she was still holding Holly's hand until she saw Linda's eyes widen slightly. She felt Holly tense beside her, a faint blush coloring her cheeks, but she didn't pull her hand away. Instead, she met her mother's gaze steadily, a silent challenge in her eyes.

The moment stretched, and Mack held her breath, wondering if Linda was about to lose it entirely. But she simply gave her a small nod, so subtle Mack almost missed it, before turning back to face the front.

Outside, the landscape began to change, the vast open fields giving way to more frequent clusters of buildings as they approached the outskirts of Minneapolis. Sprawling suburbia began to replace the open fields, with neat rows of houses and manicured lawns peeking out from under blankets of snow. Strip malls and gas stations dotted the roadside, their parking lots bustling with last-minute Christmas shoppers. As they drew closer to the city center, the skyline came into view, a collection of glass and steel structures rising up against the pale winter sky. The iconic Foshay Tower stood out among the more modern buildings, a testament to the city's history amidst its growth. Traffic began to thicken, brake lights glowing red as they merged onto the freeway leading into downtown Minneapolis. The Mississippi River snaked alongside them, its waters dark and choppy, partially frozen in places.

Twenty minutes later, Mack's phone buzzed again. "Mom says Sarah's pushing," she announced, her voice a mix of excitement and nervous energy.

Linda let out a small gasp. "Oh my! Peter, how much longer?"

Peter glanced at the GPS on the dashboard. "About twelve minutes to the hospital, traffic permitting."

"We'll make it," Holly said softly, giving Mack's hand another reassuring squeeze. "And even if we don't, you'll be there soon after. That's what matters."

Mack nodded, trying to calm her racing heart. "You're right. I just... I promised Sarah I'd be there."

"And you will be," Holly assured her. "Maybe not for the actual birth, but for all the important moments after.

The first time she holds the baby, the first feeding, the first diaper change..."

"Oh God," Mack groaned, a nervous laugh escaping her. "I didn't even think about diapers. I don't know the first thing about changing a diaper and I'm staying with her for two weeks to help her out."

Linda turned around again, her earlier nervousness replaced by a warm smile. "Peter was so nervous about changing Holly's diaper for the first time that he put it on backward. Well, I can tell you, he learned his lesson because Holly sure liked her food, and she—"

"Mom!" Holly exclaimed, her cheeks flushing pink.

Peter chuckled from the driver's seat. "Yes, that's a mistake you only make once."

The car filled with laughter, the tension of the moment broken. Despite the unconventional circumstances, Mack felt welcomed by Holly's family in a way she hadn't expected. She watched as other familiar landmarks began to appear—the glass skyscrapers of downtown Minneapolis, the distinctive shape of the US Bank Stadium, and finally, the hospital.

As Peter pulled up to the main entrance, Mack felt a sudden reluctance to let go of Holly's hand. These past two days had been a whirlwind, and Holly had become an unexpected anchor in the chaos. The thought of facing this momentous occasion without her by her side felt daunting.

Holly seemed to sense her hesitation. "Do you want me to come in with you?" she asked softly. "Not into the delivery room, of course, but I can wait outside."

Mack nodded. "Would you? I mean, if it's okay with your parents..."

"Of course, dear," Linda said. "We'll find parking and wait for Holly."

"Thank you." Mack placed a hand on Linda's shoulder. "For everything. I'll ask Holly for your details so I can thank you properly."

As she and Holly climbed out of the car, she smiled when Holly took her hand again, and they headed inside and down the hallway, following the signs to the delivery rooms.

She skidded to a stop in front of the nurses' station, slightly out of breath.

"I'm looking for Sarah Harper," she managed to say between pants. "I'm her sister."

The nurse nodded, quickly checking her computer. "Room 305, just down the hall on your left."

Mack barely had time to say thank you before she was off again, her eyes scanning the room numbers as she passed —301...303...305. Leaving Holly outside, she burst through the door, her entrance causing everyone in the room to look up. Sarah lay on the bed, her face flushed and hair plastered to her forehead with sweat. Their parents stood on either side of her.

"Mack!" Sarah exclaimed, her voice strained but filled with relief. "You made it!"

Mack rushed to her sister's side, taking her hand. "Of course I did. I promised, didn't I?"

The midwife, positioned at the foot of the bed, looked up. "Hello, Mack. Perfect timing."

The next few minutes were a blur of activity. Mack was counting with the midwife, encouraging her sister, and trying not to wince as Sarah squeezed her hand with surprising strength. "One more big push, Sarah," the midwife said. "The baby's almost here!"

Sarah gritted her teeth, bearing down with all her might. Mack held her breath, her eyes fixed on the midwife.

She fumbled under the covers and then, suddenly, a cry filled the room—strong and indignant, announcing the arrival of new life.

"It's a girl!" the midwife announced, holding up the squirming, wailing infant.

Mack felt tears spring to her eyes as she watched the midwife place the baby on Sarah's chest. Her niece—red-faced, wrinkled, and absolutely perfect.

"Hi there, little one," Sarah whispered, her voice thick with emotion. "We've been waiting for you."

Mack leaned in, marveling at the tiny fingers, the tuft of dark hair, the way the baby's cries quieted as she nestled against her mother's skin.

"She's beautiful, Sarah," Mack whispered. "You did amazing."

Sarah looked up at her, eyes shining with tears and exhaustion. "I'm so glad you're here, Sis. Isn't she perfect?" Mack watched as Sarah cradled her newborn daughter, marveling at how naturally her sister took to motherhood. Despite the exhaustion evident on her face, Sarah's eyes shone with love and wonder as she gazed at the tiny bundle in her arms. The baby, still pink and wrinkled, had already stopped crying and was blinking up at her mother with unfocused eyes.

"Sarah, you're a natural," Mack said softly, gently stroking her niece's tiny hand. She only then realized she was crying, and so were her parents, who stood huddled over them in awe.

"I...I need to step out for just a moment. Holly's waiting in the hallway, and I want to say goodbye and get her parents' number so I can thank them for getting me here."

Sarah didn't seem to hear her, she was solely focused on her baby, but Mack's mother looked up, a knowing smile on her tired face. "Holly? Is that the woman you shared the motel room with?"

"Yeah...I'll tell you all about it later. I'll be right back, okay?"

With a final squeeze of her sister's hand, Mack slipped out into the hallway. She spotted Holly immediately, pacing nervously near the waiting area. "Everything okay?"

"It's a girl," Mack announced as she approached Holly. "She's perfect, Holly. Absolutely perfect."

Without hesitation, Holly pulled her into a tight embrace. "Congratulations, Aunt Mack," she murmured, her breath warm against Mack's ear. She pulled away and gave her a beaming smile. "I don't want to hold you up. Go be with your family." She held out her phone. "Just give me your number. We'll catch up later."

Chapter 18

Holly

As they pulled into the familiar driveway, a wave of nostalgia washed over Holly. The two-story colonial house where she grew up stood before them, looking exactly as it had for the past thirty years. The redbrick exterior, the white shutters framing each window, the neatly trimmed hedges lining the front walkway—it was all just as she remembered.

Holly took a deep breath, steeling herself as she stepped out of the car. The cold Minnesota air nipped at her cheeks, a stark contrast to the warmth she'd felt just hours ago in Mack's arms. She pushed the thought aside, reminding herself to focus on the present moment. This reunion with her parents was too important to be distracted.

"Welcome home, sweetheart," her mom said, coming around the car to give her another hug. Her embrace was tentative, as if she was afraid Holly might pull away. Holly leaned into it, trying to convey without words that she was here, that she wanted this to work.

Her dad was already at the trunk, pulling out her bag. "I'll take this inside," he said, and Holly noticed the slight stoop to his shoulders that wasn't there the last time she visited.

They headed inside and the scent of cinnamon and pine enveloped her. Her mom had always gone all out with the Christmas decorations, and this year was no exception. Garlands draped the staircase banister, twinkling lights framed the windows, and a massive Christmas tree dominated the corner of the living room.

"You've outdone yourself this year, Mom," Holly said, taking in the festive atmosphere.

Her mom gave a small smile. "Well, I wanted everything to be perfect for your visit."

The words hung in the air between them, laden with unspoken hope and fear. Holly swallowed hard, pushing down the lump forming in her throat. "It looks wonderful."

She followed her mom into the kitchen, and her eyes were drawn to the refrigerator. There, held by a faded magnet shaped like a smiling sun, was a drawing she had made when she was six years old. The crayon lines were faded now, but she could still make out the stick figure family—Mom, Dad, and herself, holding hands under a rainbow. The paper was yellowed with age, the edges slightly curled. Yet here it was, still proudly displayed after all these years. It was such a small thing, but it spoke volumes about the love and hope that had always been present in this house, even when words failed them.

When Holly traced the outlines of the drawing, her mom came to stand beside her. "It's one of my favorite things you've ever made."

Holly's gaze drifted to the hallway, where she could see the door to her old bedroom. She didn't need to open it to know what was inside. The last time she slept there, it was like stepping back in time—the same pink sheets on the bed, the shelf still lined with her old Nancy Drew mysteries. It was as if that room had been frozen in time, waiting for the girl she used to be to return.

Her mom placed a gentle hand on her arm. "It's so good to have you back, Holly."

Holly turned to her, seeing the mix of love and uncertainty in her eyes. "It's good to be back," she replied, meaning it more than she expected to.

"Why don't we make some coffee?" her mom suggested. "Your father's settling in the living room to rest after the drive."

Holly nodded, grateful for the familiar routine. As she filled the coffeemaker, her mom bustled around, pulling mugs from the cupboard, and brought out homemade cookies that smelled like they were baked last night. It was a dance they'd performed countless times over the years, and Holly found comfort in the steps.

When she opened the fridge to grab the milk, Holly was faced with a beautifully decorated cake on one shelf, while a large turkey took up most of the bottom compartment. Various side dishes in clear containers were stacked neatly, ready to be heated.

"Christmas dinner?" she asked, a lump forming in her throat. Despite their strained relationship over the past year, they had prepared everything, hoping she would come home.

Her mom nodded. "What time do you want to eat?"

Holly hesitated, remembering all the Christmas Eves spent at the candlelight service, Christmas mornings singing carols and listening to the familiar story of Jesus' birth. It had always been a cornerstone of their family traditions, but now... "That depends. Were you planning on eating before or after church?"

"Maybe this year, we can skip church and just catch up?" her mom said.

Holly blinked, stunned by the suggestion. "Are you sure?" She searched her mom's face for any sign of reluctance but found none.

"Yes. I've discussed it with your father. We have a lot to catch up on and talk about, and we don't want to waste any more time."

Tears pricked at the corners of Holly's eyes. This simple gesture meant more to her than she could express. "I'd like that."

So much had happened in the past few days—meeting Mack, their whirlwind connection, and now this unexpected olive branch from her parents, who genuinely seemed to be trying to accept who she was. It was overwhelming but in the best possible way.

They carried their mugs of coffee into the living room, where her dad was sitting in his favorite armchair by the fireplace. He looked up as they entered, a tentative smile on his face.

"So, Holly," he said, "tell us about your work. How are things at the firm?"

Holly sat on the couch next to her mom and launched into a description of her latest case, grateful for the safe topic. As she talked, she could see her parents hanging on every word, genuinely interested in her life. It was nothing like their last conversation, where every word felt like it was being scrutinized and judged.

They continued to talk about her work, about the latest gossip from church—which her mom filled her in on despite their decision to skip the service—about her dad's golf game and her mom's book club. It was all very normal, very familiar, and yet there was an undercurrent of something new—an openness, a willingness to listen and understand.

Eventually, there was a lull in the conversation. Holly knew they were all thinking about the elephant in the room.

"Mom, Dad," she began. "Thank you for coming to get me. I know things have been...difficult between us."

They exchanged a glance, and her mom reached out to take her hand. "We love you, Holly," she said softly. "We always have, and we always will. We may not understand everything, but we want to try."

Her dad leaned forward in his chair. "Your mother and I have done a lot of talking, a lot of praying. We...we weren't fair to you before. We let our fears and our preconceptions cloud our judgment. And we're sorry for that."

Holly felt tears welling up in her eyes, but she blinked them back. "It's okay," she said. "It was a shock for you. Maybe I should have handled it better."

"No," her mom said firmly. "You were brave to tell us, and we should have supported you from the start. We're your parents. That's our job. Unfortunately, we didn't realize what damage we'd done until we feared we'd lost you."

A tear escaped, rolling down Holly's cheek. "I've missed you both so much," she whispered.

Her dad stood up abruptly, crossing the room to sit on her other side. He put an arm around her shoulders, pulling her close. "We've missed you too, sweetheart," he said, his voice thick with emotion.

For a moment, they just sat there, the three of them huddled together on the couch. Relief washed over Holly in waves, mingled with a tentative hope that she'd been afraid to nurture for so long. The warmth of her parents' embrace, the sincerity in their words—it was everything she'd longed for since that fateful day she came out to them. Yet, beneath the joy, there was still a whisper of fear. Could it really be this easy? Would their acceptance last when faced with the reality of her life, of potentially dating someone like Mack? But as she felt her father's strong arm around her and her mother's hand in hers, Holly chose to silence that doubt, at least for now. This moment, this tentative reconciliation, felt like a fragile, precious gift. And as she blinked back tears, she realized that for the first time in a long time, she felt like she was truly home—not just in this house, but in her parents' hearts.

Chapter 19

Mack

Mack sat in a nursing chair, cradling her newborn niece, Isabel, while her parents and sister dug into the Thai takeout spread across the small overbed table.

Isabel's tiny fingers curled around Mack's pinky, her grip surprisingly strong for someone not even a day old. Mack couldn't tear her eyes away from the perfect little face nestled against her chest. Ten hours had passed since Isabel's dramatic entrance into the world, and Mack still felt like she was floating in a bubble of wonder and exhaustion.

"Mack, are you sure you don't want any pad Thai?" her mother asked, holding out a plastic fork laden with noodles.

Mack shook her head, smiling. "I'm good, Mom. I'll eat in a bit. You guys enjoy."

Sarah let out a massive yawn, fork paused halfway to her mouth. "God, I'm so tired," she mumbled. "But so hungry." She shoved the bite of green curry into her mouth, eyes closing in bliss. "This is amazing. I've been craving Thai for days." She took another bite, this time of the papaya salad. "I was so worried about eating spicy food," she said between chews. "I kept thinking it might kick-start labor before you got here, Mack."

"Well, I'm glad you waited," Mack replied, gently stroking Isabel's cheek. "I wouldn't have missed this for the world."

Her phone buzzed on the arm of the chair, and Mack's heart did a little flip. She knew without looking that it was Holly. They'd been texting on and off all day, between Isabel's feeds and Sarah's naps. Mack tried not to message too often, knowing Holly was having an important reunion with her parents, but every time she did, Holly replied almost immediately.

"Is that Holly?" her mother asked.

Mack felt a blush creep up her neck. "Yeah. She's just checking in."

"Holly?" Sarah perked up, suddenly more alert. "The cute lawyer you were stranded with? Oh, I need details."

"There's not much to tell. We just...connected." Mack said, aiming for nonchalance but failing miserably.

"Connected enough for her parents to drive you three hours to the hospital on Christmas Day?" her father asked.

Mack shrugged, feeling oddly shy. It was strange to be discussing her love life—or whatever this thing with Holly was—with her family while holding her newborn niece. "They were very kind. I got lucky."

"Mmm," Sarah hummed, a mischievous glint in her eye despite her exhaustion. "I bet you did."

"Sarah!" Mack chuckled. "There's a baby present!"

"Oh please, it will be years before we have to start watching our words." Sarah waved a hand. "Besides, I just pushed a human out of my body. I'm allowed to be a little inappropriate."

Mack shook her head with an amused grin, and carefully shifted Isabel to one arm so she could check her phone. This time, the message from Holly wasn't just text. It was a picture of a beautifully set dinner table, resplendent with fine china, sparkling crystal, and elegant centerpieces. In the background, Mack could make out a cozy living room, a Christmas tree twinkling in the corner. Underneath, a message said, *Happy Christmas.*

Mack smiled. She was so happy for Holly, knowing how nervous she'd been about reconnecting with her parents. This picture spoke volumes about how well things must be going. She adjusted her position in the chair, angling herself and Isabel toward the light. Holding up her phone, she tried to get both of them in frame and took a selfie. She sent it off to Holly with a message: *Merry Christmas from Aunt Mack and Isabel! Hope you're having a wonderful time with your family.*

As she waited for Holly's response, Mack found herself reflecting on the whirlwind of the past few days. It felt surreal to be sitting here, holding her newborn niece, after all the chaos of being stranded in Watertown. And Holly... Mack's heart fluttered at the thought of her. Their connection had been so unexpected, so intense. Part of her still couldn't believe it was real.

Her phone buzzed again, pulling her from her reverie. Holly's reply was swift and enthusiastic: *Oh my god, she's absolutely precious! You look so natural holding her. Give her a kiss from me. Things are going really well here—I'll call you tomorrow to fill you in and I want to hear all about your niece.*

A wide grin spread across Mack's face as she read Holly's message. She pressed a gentle kiss to Isabel's forehead, whispering, "That one's from Holly."

"You've got it bad, Sis," Sarah, who had been watching

her, said dryly. She yawned again, her eyelids drooping. "As much as I want to hear all about your blossoming romance, I think I need to sleep for about a year."

"Of course, honey," their mother said, immediately switching into caretaker mode. She began clearing away the takeout containers and prepared a plate for Mack, their father helping to tidy up the small room.

Mack stood carefully. "I'll put Isabel in the bassinet," she whispered, moving toward the clear plastic crib next to Sarah's bed. As she gently laid her down, Mack marveled again at how tiny she was. Her little fists were curled up near her face, her chest rising and falling with each breath. Mack felt a surge of protectiveness wash over her. She may have only known Isabel for a few hours, but she already loved her niece fiercely.

"Sleep tight, little one," she murmured, tucking the blanket around Isabel, then turned back to find Sarah sleeping.

"We're going to head home for a bit," her mother whispered. "Get some rest at home, honey. We'll be back in a few hours."

Mack nodded, giving each of them a hug. "Thanks for everything," she said. "I think I'll stay here a while longer and have some food, if that's okay."

Her father patted her on the back. "Of course. Call if you need anything."

As the door closed behind them, the room fell quiet, and Mack sank back into the armchair with a plate of green curry and rice. She was exhausted and had been running on adrenaline and coffee, but she couldn't bring herself to leave just yet.

She realized how blessed she truly was. This Christmas had given her not one, but two precious gifts—the miracle of new life in her niece, and the promise of new love with Holly. Through the window, she saw a gentle snowfall begin outside, blanketing the city in a fresh layer of white. Streetlights cast a warm glow on the fresh powder, making it sparkle like countless tiny diamonds. Nature was hitting the reset button, offering a clean slate for new beginnings.

She thought about the perfectly wrapped presents for her family that had been sitting in her hallway for a week, the carefully curated playlist of Christmas songs, the recipe for eggnog she'd been meaning to try. All those preparations seemed trivial now, paling in comparison to the sight of Isabel before her and the flutter in her chest every time her phone lit up with a message from Holly. The irony wasn't lost on her—her meticulous holiday plans had unraveled into a beautiful chaos.

Isabel whimpered softly. Mack set her plate to the side and gently placed a hand on Isabel's tummy. The baby settled at her touch, her face relaxing back into sleep. She watched her niece, struck by the perfection of this quiet moment, and a profound sense of peace washed over her. She was exactly where she was meant to be.

Chapter 20

Holly

The warm glow of candles flickered across the dining room table, casting dancing shadows on the walls. Holly stood, gathering the last of the dessert plates, a contentment settling over her that she hadn't felt in this house for a long time.

"Thank you both for dinner," she said, smiling at her parents. "It was wonderful."

Her mother beamed, the lines around her eyes crinkling with genuine happiness. "We're just so glad you're here, sweetheart."

Her father nodded in agreement, a soft smile playing on his lips. "It's been a perfect Christmas."

As they stood, her mother stifled a yawn, and Holly felt a surge of affection for her. The day had been filled with tentative steps toward reconciliation, moments of laughter, and even a few tears. It wasn't perfect—there were still awkward pauses and careful navigation of certain topics—but it was progress. More than she'd dared to hope for.

"We should head to bed," her father said, glancing at the ornate clock on the mantel. "It's been a long day."

Holly nodded, but hesitated, her heart quickening. "Actually, before you go...would it be all right if I borrowed the car?"

Her parents exchanged a glance. "Of course," her mother said. "But where are you going at this hour?"

Holly took a deep breath, steeling herself. Just a week ago, the idea of mentioning a female love interest to her parents had seemed impossible. But they had surprised her today, even bringing up Mack over dinner, commenting on how nice she seemed.

"I...I was hoping to go see Mack at the hospital," Holly said, the words tumbling out in a rush. "I know it's late, but I just...I want to check on her, see how she's doing."

There was a moment of silence, and Holly felt her chest tighten. But then her father's face softened, and he pointed to the sideboard, where his car keys were.

"Say hello from us. Just drive safely, all right? The roads might be icy."

Holly blinked, momentarily stunned. "I will, Dad. Thank you."

Her mother stepped forward, enveloping her in a warm hug. "Yes. Tell Mack we said hello," she murmured. "And congratulations again on becoming an aunt."

As Holly slipped on her coat and headed out, she felt a lightness in her step that had been missing for far too long. The car's engine purred to life, and she pulled out of the driveway, the familiar streets of her childhood neighborhood sliding by in a blur of twinkling Christmas lights.

As she merged onto the highway, a nervous flutter began in her belly, growing stronger with each mile that brought her closer to the hospital. Holly wasn't entirely sure why it felt so important to see Mack tonight. They had been texting throughout the day, sharing updates and well-wishes. But somehow, it wasn't enough.

Perhaps it was the symbolism of it all, Holly mused as she navigated through the light evening traffic. They had started Christmas together, strangers thrown together by circumstance. Now, as the holiday drew to a close, Holly felt an inexplicable pull to end it together.

The city lights glowed softly against the night sky, a gentle snowfall adding a dreamlike quality to the scene. Holly's mind wandered back to their time in Watertown. It felt like a lifetime ago, yet also as if no time had passed at all.

When she arrived at the hospital, Holly's heart began to race, a mix of excitement and nervousness coursing through her veins. She found a parking spot and sat for a moment, gathering her courage before she dialed Mack's number.

"Holly? Is everything okay?"

"Everything's fine," Holly assured her quickly. "I'm actually... I'm here. At the hospital."

There was a beat of silence, and then Mack's voice, filled with disbelief and joy. "You're here? Now?"

"Yeah," Holly said, a smile spreading across her face. "Can you come down? I'm in the parking lot."

"I'll be right there," Mack replied, and Holly could hear the smile in her voice.

Holly stepped out of the car, the cold air nipping at her cheeks as she made her way toward the hospital entrance. Her eyes scanned the area, searching for a glimpse of teal hair in the sea of cars and late-night visitors.

And then, there she was. Mack burst through the sliding doors, her eyes wild and searching until they locked onto Holly. For a moment, they both stood frozen, drinking in the sight of each other.

Then, as if pulled by some invisible force, Holly's feet

carried her forward, her pace quickening with each step until she was practically running. Mack matched her stride for stride, and they collided in the middle of the walkway, arms wrapping tightly around each other.

Holly buried her face in the crook of Mack's neck, breathing in her scent. She felt Mack's arms tighten around her waist, pulling her impossibly closer.

"I can't believe you're here," Mack whispered, her breath warm against Holly's ear.

Holly pulled back just enough to meet Mack's gaze, her heart swelling at the joy and wonder she saw reflected there. Without a word, she leaned in, capturing Mack's lips in a kiss.

It felt like coming home to a place Holly had never known existed. Mack's lips were soft yet insistent, and she marveled at how familiar this felt, how right, despite the newness of it all. Her fingers traced the curve of Mack's jaw, committing every detail to memory—the smoothness of her skin, the delicate hollow beneath her ear, the pulse that fluttered beneath her fingertips. The comfort of Mack's embrace, the way their bodies fit together, it all felt too perfect to be mere coincidence.

As she lost herself in the kiss, Holly's mind wandered to the chain of events that had brought them here—a snowstorm, a crowded airport, a shortage of motel rooms. What were the odds? Had the universe conspired to bring them together? Holly had never been one for grand notions of fate or destiny, but in this moment, with Mack's arms around her, she found herself reconsidering.

As they slowly pulled apart, their eyes locked, both of them slightly breathless. Mack broke the silence first, her voice soft and uncertain. "So...where do we go from here?"

Holly's lips curved into a smile. "You know, this might

sound crazy, but I can't shake this feeling that we were meant to meet. Like all those little coincidences weren't really coincidences at all."

"Yeah. I've been thinking the same thing, and..." Mack paused. "If I'm honest, I missed you today and with every minute that passed, I wanted to see you more." She took a deep breath. "Look...I don't know exactly where we're going, but I know I want to go there with you."

Holly felt a rush of emotion as she took Mack's hands and laced their fingers together. "I'd like that," she whispered. Their eyes met again, and in that moment, surrounded by the soft glow of hospital lights and gently falling snow, she embraced the prospect of new beginnings. In the blue depths of Mack's eyes, she saw a universe of possibilities—laughter shared over morning coffee, quiet nights spent reading side by side, and many more Christmases to come...

Perhaps there was some greater force at work, guiding them toward each other, or perhaps it was simply the magic of the season, turning strangers into soulmates in the span of a few snow-filled days.

"Merry Christmas, girlfriend," Holly murmured.

Mack laughed softly, the sound warming Holly from the inside out. "Merry Christmas, girlfriend."

Epilogue – Mack

Mack tried to wiggle her way out of Maude Mistletoe's enthusiastic embrace, but the older woman's grip was surprisingly strong.

"Oh, it's so wonderful to see you two again!" Maude exclaimed, finally releasing Mack only to immediately pull Holly into an equally exuberant hug. "And together! You know, I've always had a knack for putting the right people in the right room at the right time. It's a gift. And you two... well, let's just say I had a feeling about you from the start and the Mistletoe Motel works in mysterious ways."

Mack chuckled, both at Maude's crazy statement and at the sight of Holly's slightly overwhelmed expression as she was enveloped in Maude's arms. A year had passed since they'd been stranded in Watertown, forced to share a room at the Mistletoe Motel. Now here they were, back again by choice to celebrate their anniversary. It wasn't the most romantic choice for a getaway, but it certainly felt fitting and even oddly romantic.

Mack took in the motel lobby. Nothing had changed.

Epilogue – Mack

The same over-the-top Christmas decorations covered every available surface, strings of twinkling lights crisscrossed the ceiling, and tinsel garlands framed every doorway and window. And then there was Maude herself, resplendent in a Christmas sweater that put all others to shame. This year's creation featured a three-dimensional Christmas tree, complete with actual tiny ornaments dangling from the knitted branches.

"We're so happy to be back," Holly said, reaching for Mack's hand and giving it a squeeze. "We couldn't think of a better place than Watertown to celebrate our anniversary."

Mack nodded in agreement. Although it wasn't the most comfortable option, there was something undeniably charming about the Mistletoe Motel, with all its kitschy glory, and it held a special place in their hearts now.

"Oh, you two are just the sweetest," Maude gushed. She bustled behind the reception desk, rummaging through a drawer. "Now, let me just find your key. I've got you in Room Fifteen again—I assumed you'd want the same room? I saw your name on the reservation, Holly, so I made sure to keep that one free for you. Now, I should warn you, we haven't quite gotten around to renovating that room yet. But don't you worry, we've made sure to tape off those peep-holes this time."

"That's perfect, thank you," Holly said, while Mack tried not to think too hard about the state of that particular room.

"It's no trouble at all, dear," Maude said as if she'd done them a favor. "I noticed you're only staying the one night. Are you sure you don't want to extend your stay? There's no storm this year, so we're having a special Christmas Eve

Epilogue - Mack

bonfire in town tomorrow night, complete with s'mores and hot cocoa!"

"That sounds lovely, Maude, but we really do need to head back tomorrow," Holly explained. "We drove here to make sure we'd be able to spend Christmas with our families this year."

"And it's my niece's first birthday," Mack added. "Can't miss that."

"Oh, of course!" Maude spread her arms. "Family is so important, especially at Christmas. And a first birthday! How exciting. Did you manage to get there in time last year? Holly told me you were in a rush when she came to check out."

"I did." Mack smiled, a warm feeling spreading through her chest at the thought of Isabel. She and Holly had become regular babysitters for Sarah, and she loved spending time with the little bundle of joy. "She's so big now, I can hardly believe it's been a year already."

"My, how time flies," Maude mused. "So what are the plans?"

"We're spending Christmas Eve with Holly's parents," Mack said. "And Christmas Day with mine."

"That sounds lovely. Well, we're just tickled that you chose to spend your anniversary with us. We've had a beautiful fresh layer of snow overnight, but the weather's supposed to be good for your drive back tomorrow."

"Yes, we made sure to check the forecast before we left," Holly said humorously. She held up the key and shot Maude a beaming smile. "Well, we'd better go and freshen up before we head out for our date night at Marty's diner."

"You do that, dear." Maude winked. "Enjoy your date night and say hi to Marty from me!"

Epilogue - Mack

Holly giggled as they headed out and walked toward their room. "She's so sweet. Isn't it fun to be back?"

"It's wonderful." Mack pulled her in to kiss her temple. "And I love going anywhere with you. Even the Mistletoe Motel," she joked. A wave of nostalgia washed over her as they stepped into Room Fifteen. So much had changed in the past year, and yet being here made it feel like no time had passed at all. She'd expected that at least their modified wall art had been painted over, but even that was still there. "Wow..."

"Updates are clearly not their priority." Holly laughed. "Decorations over renovations, that should be their tagline." She and Holly exchanged an amused glance before simultaneously looking up. There, hanging from the ceiling, was a large sprig of mistletoe.

"Well," Mack said, a slow grin spreading across her face. "I guess the Mistletoe traditions haven't changed either."

Holly laughed and closed the distance between them. "And we shouldn't break tradition. That would be bad luck." She wrapped her arms around Mack's waist, pulling her close, and their lips met in a kiss that was both familiar and thrilling.

Mack could never get enough of kissing Holly, even now that they'd moved in together and shared countless intimate moments. Each kiss still held that spark of excitement from their first night together in this very room. As they broke apart, Mack gazed into Holly's eyes. They had grown so close over the past year. The initial attraction had blossomed into a love stronger than anything she'd ever experienced. Somehow, in this bizarre place, she'd found the love of her life, and Mack marveled at how a series of inconveniences had led to the greatest convenience of all—finding her perfect match in Holly.

Epilogue – Mack

"Happy anniversary, princess," she murmured. "I love you."

Holly giggled at the old nickname that Mack refused to give up. Some things never changed, and they weren't supposed to. "Happy anniversary, babe." She cupped Mack's face and kissed her again. "I love you too."

Afterword

I hope you've loved reading Mistletoe Motel as much as I've loved writing it. If you've enjoyed this book, would you consider rating it and reviewing it? Reviews are very important to authors and I'd be really grateful!

About the Author

Lise Gold is an author of lesbian romance. Her romantic attitude, enthusiasm for travel and love for feel good stories form the heartland of her writing. Born in London to a Norwegian mother and English father, and growing up between the UK, Norway, Zambia and the Netherlands, she feels at home pretty much everywhere and has an unending curiosity for new destinations. She goes by 'write what you know' and is often found in exotic locations doing research or getting inspired for her next novel.

Working as a designer for fifteen years and singing semi-professionally, Lise has always been a creative at heart. Her novels are the result of a quest for a new passion after resigning from her design job in 2018.

When not writing from her kitchen table, Lise can be found cooking, at the gym or singing her heart out somewhere, preferably country or blues. She lives in London with her dogs El Comandante and Bubba.

Sign up to her newsletter: https://bit.ly/2GclQzf

Also by Lise Gold

Lily's Fire

Beyond the Skyline

The Cruise

French Summer

Fireflies

Northern Lights

Southern Roots

Eastern Nights

Western Shores

Northern Vows

Living

The Scent of Rome

Blue

The Next Life

In The Mirror

Christmas In Heaven

Welcome to Paradise

After Sunset

Paradise Pride

Cupid Is A Cat

Members Only

Along The Mystic River

In Dreams

Chance Encounters

Songbirds of Sedona

Red Rock Ranch

Under the pen name Madeleine Taylor

The Good Girl

Online

Masquerade

Santa's Favorite

Spanish translations by Rocío T. Fernández

Verano Francés

Vivir

Nada Más Que Azul

Luciérnagas

Solo Para Socios

German translations by Iris Pilzer

Members Only: Nur für Mitglieder

Hindi translations

Zindagi